MANGO CAKE AND MURDER

CHRISTY MURPHY

D1526307

Copyright © 2016 by Christy Murphy

All rights reserved.

No part of this book may be reproduced in any form or by any electronic or mechanical means, including information storage and retrieval systems, without written permission from the author, except for the use of brief quotations in a book review.

Cover illustrator, Edie Murphy.

Cover design, Priscilla Pantin

Editor, Robb Fulcher

This book is a work of fiction. Names, characters, places, and incidents are the products of the author's imagination or used fictitiously. Any resemblance to the actual events, locales or persons, living or dead, is entirely coincidental.

Join Mom & Christy's Cozy Mysteries Club. You'll find out how to get free advanced copies of new cozies, special discounts, fun extras (like cute pics of the cat that inspired Moriarty), and more.

Join Mom & Christy's Cozy Mysteries Club

Click or copy and paste this link into your browser:

http://christymurphy.com/club

To my family

Mom, Dad, David, Edie, David, Diana, and Darwin

And the next generation of Murphys: Jason, Anthony, and Ana

M om and I were told we'd be catering a gathering of twenty-five, but so far there were only eight people. Three of the guests, who'd come in the same car and had just arrived, were already making excuses to leave. They claimed they had to "wake up early." It was only 4:15 in the afternoon.

Margaret, the sixty-year-old hostess, had run out of exciting party conversation once she'd pitched all the guests on her latest venture, a memorial pet taxidermy service. "I know what we need," she said, guessing that her dead pet talk wasn't enough to kick the party into high gear. "Let's have some music!" She walked over to what looked like a sideboard and opened a wooden door revealing a large, antiquated CD player.

Four fumble-filled minutes later the Bee Gees' song "Tragedy" echoed throughout the large living room. The Gibb brothers sang in gleeful harmony about the difficulties of a life going nowhere when no one loves you. I served the bored partygoers crab rangoon and thought about my impending divorce.

Every guest, even though most were on medication that probably warned them not to drink, made their way over to Mom at the bar. Mom served up her signature drink, The Filipino Fling, a twist on the Singapore Sling. Mom's concoction mixed gin, cherry brandy, lemon juice, and a splash of Mom's special sauce—a rich sugar syrup that would skyrocket a person's glucose levels if swallowed on its own.

"Tragedy" ended and the CD shuffled over to another tune, "You Should Be Dancing." The guests, having just started work on their Flings, dismissed the well-harmonized advice. I hoped the drinks would kick in soon. This party needed some serious flinging.

Margaret looked over to me and made an awkward boogie my way. I could see the worried hostess look in her blue eyes. "I think it's time for the guest of honor to make an appearance," she said. "It'll liven up the party. Would you mind fetching Father from the study?"

It's a sad party when the surly, eighty-five-year-old "birthday boy" is the big hope for making an occasion festive.

"Right away," I answered hoping to sound upbeat and took my nearly-full serving tray to the kitchen. I set the platter down on the expensive marble counter and relieved the awkward party tension with a stolen bite of a crab rangoon. It was so good I snagged two more and ate them as I made my way up the back-stairs and down the hall. The heavy, wood door to the den was closed. I brushed the rangoon dust off on my apron and knocked. No answer. I waited a minute and knocked louder. The Bee Gees continued to blare from downstairs. I figured Margaret's dad didn't hear me through the thick door and the music.

"Mr. Sanders," I said as I eased open the door. I didn't want to startle him. As I entered, my shoe slipped on something. I lifted my foot and discovered a small capsule crushed under my heel.

That's when I noticed pills scattered everywhere, and Harold Sanders lying on the floor. The desk chair and lamp were knocked over. I rushed to his side, rolled him on his back, and checked to see if he was breathing. No luck. I started CPR and yelled for help, to no avail.

Grabbing my cell from my apron pocket, I dialed 911, and hit the speaker button. I waited for the call to connect and continued CPR. There was silence as the CD player chose another song. I informed the 911 operator about the situation. She dispatched an ambulance, and I kept up my efforts to revive Mr. Sanders. The upbeat, Travolta-strolling riff of "Staying Alive" pulsated from downstairs.

As I tried to stay positive, I caught the Brothers Gibb singing about going nowhere again. I'd never realized until that day how depressing Bee Gee songs could be. And no matter how many times the group ah, ah, ah-ed about Staying Alive, Mr. Sanders, like the guests downstairs, ignored their harmonious advice.

I'd imagined Mom and my's first catering gig together

couldn't get worse when the guest of honor died. But later, we found out Harold Sanders had been murdered.

––––––––

I THOUGHT THIS STAGE OF MY LIFE WAS GOING TO be the "Oh no! I'm a broke, 35 year-old woman getting out of a bad relationship and moving back with my mother" stage. But instead, it was more like "I'm half of a mother-daughter catering/crime-solving team" and life has never been better. Who knew?

Sure, my life must've been in a pretty depressing place for crime and murder to make things better. But who am I to judge Fate? People ask me (Alright, one person asked me, and most people ask Mom), "How did you two begin solving crimes?"

I'd love to say our journey began some place exciting, like on an express train through Europe or aboard an Egyptian river cruise, but it started in a place a great deal more modest and a lot more greasy.

Insert dreamy flashback music ...

Mom sat across from me and surveyed the once-white tiles that lined the walls of Pete's Burger. The place looked dirty when I'd first come to work here, but now, the fast food joint seemed to grow an extra layer of grime under Mom's scrutiny.

"Let's get out of here, kid. This place is lousy," she said.

I signaled for her to speak more quietly. Mom had a high-pitched voice that carried. "My boss is right there," I said, and pointed to "Mr. Stephens" leaning on the counter a few yards from our dilapidated, vinyl-padded booth. He insisted on being called "Mr. Stephens" despite the fact that he was in his twenties, and I was likely a decade older than him.

"Don't worry. I'm a customer, he'll ignore me," Mom whispered.

I laughed. The singular table of customers and my new boss turned to look. I quieted myself and tried to wipe the grease off my glasses, as if nothing had happened. After smearing the grease around for a minute, I pushed my glasses back onto my round face and sighed. This place was lousy, and the polyester uniform I had to wear didn't help. At least Mom had stopped by to visit me on my break.

When I was a kid, I never noticed Mom had a Filipino accent. But as I spent more time away from home, I missed her familiar lilt, complete with the "d" sound in the place the "th" usually inhabited. Words like "this" and "these" sounded closer to "dis" and "dese" as in "dis place is lousy."

I watched Mom push her salad around with her fork. My petite mom wasn't a big eater, but I could tell, even if she were starving, she wouldn't eat that salad.

"How do they make salad greasy?" Mom asked.

"You don't like the Prime Burger Salad?"

"Ah!" Mom scoffed and shook her head. "How fancy," she said and laughed her quiet laugh. Her eyes always teared up when she laughed. I smiled as I watched her dab her eyes with a napkin.

I couldn't take another bite of my burger either. I'd been living off this food for a month, and my body, despite its history of high-capacity food intake, had reached its burger limit.

"This place is like that motel you live in," she paused and looked around. "It's depressing."

"I'm depressed, so I figured this job would keep with the theme," I said, trying to make a joke.

Mom wasn't having it. She knew I had a brain that runs a little more worried and sad than most. I have this odd memory thing, where if something is traumatizing, my brain remembers every second of it. Don't even ask about the time my fly was down, and I passed gas while giving a speech in front of the entire seventh grade class.

Mom put her hand in mine. She looked so worried. "This is just temporary until I find something better," I told her.

"Good, I have something better. Let's go."

"You heard about a job for me?" I asked. I'd spent the last decade not finishing college and managing my soon to be ex-husband's music career. Not the best resume.

"The catering business is picking up," Mom said.

"Mom, I can't cook," I said.

Mom waved her hand as if that was a minor detail.

"There's so much to do," she said. I shot her a

doubtful look. Mom has a history of embellishing the truth.

"This," Mom started, then paused as she looked around. Not being able to find another word for how awful it was, she said, "is really lousy." She put down her fork, raided the nearby napkin holder, and tucked a wad of napkins into her purse. I knew she was serious about getting out of here. Napkin hoarding is what Mom does before she makes an exit.

"We can talk about it tonight," I said in a lowered voice.

Mom waved off my attempt to be quiet. "He's too busy waiting for his drug dealer to notice what you're doing."

Mom was suspicious of everybody for everything, and one of her favorites suspicions was that everybody was "on the drugs." Almost every friend or date I ever had was suspected of being "on the drugs."

"Mom, you say everyone is on drugs."

"But, I never say someone is waiting for his drug dealer."

She had me there.

"Let's go. We can go to the Lucky Dragon and eat food that won't make you break out."

At this point I realized my "cover-up makeup" wasn't as convincing as I'd hoped. Mom continued, "Wenling put a little TV in the back that we can watch while we fold wontons. It has cable and everything." Mom loved to watch all of those forensic shows on TV.

"Aren't you supposed to be seeing a client?" I asked.

"I saw them before I came here. They want someone to make food for what-you-call-it, a party when somebody dies?"

"A wake?"

"Yes, that's it. But the 'awake' is in two days for three hundred people. I told them, I can't do so big with short notice. I referred them to Oliver since sometimes he orders cakes from me," she said. I could never tell if my mother was lying. The truth and a convenient tale were delivered in the same tone and at the same speed. No difference in the pauses. Mom had zero tells. She should've been a poker player.

Mom got my attention with a light tap on the table,

and then she motioned to the door with her lips, the Filipino way of pointing.

I turned and spotted a skinny guy with long, stringy hair heading to the counter. Mr. Stephens grabbed a burger, shoved it into a bag, and then pretended to give the skinny guy change. Except, the man hadn't given my manager any money in the first place. And even though Mr. Stephens was standing behind the register, I could tell it wasn't open. "The change" had came from his pocket.

"At least he's not a thief," Mom whispered as the stringy-haired man handed Mr. Stephens a sandwich baggie of what looked like weed. My manager crammed the baggie in his pocket and beelined it to his office. The stringy-hair guy headed for the exit.

I turned back to Mom. She raised her eyebrows. He was waiting for his drug dealer. "Mom, how did you know that?"

"Just a guess."

"No, it wasn't. Tell me."

Mom shrugged and said, "He looked anxious like he was waiting for someone. He's not usually a drug person, but his shirt is all wrinkled, his eyes are baggy, and he kept staring at his wedding band and shaking his head. So he's going through some kind of breakup with his wife who usually keeps him in line. He counted his money three times since we've sat down. What kind of delivery would someone want in the middle of the afternoon that they are nervous about while working a cruddy job during a breakup?"

"It makes sense when you lay it out like that."

Mom nodded.

Then, it hit me. Mom was right–a lot.

Tons of my friends had been on drugs. They just hadn't offered me any.

If I'd listened to Mom, I wouldn't have married Robert. I'd never have dropped out of college, and I wouldn't have tried to dye my black hair blonde the night before senior yearbook pictures. Life lesson learned. It's never too late to start listening to Mom, and I decided I'd start right now.

"I'll change and get my purse," I said.

———

Worry niggled at my brain as I parked my Honda at an open meter a short block from the Lucky Dragon. Mom had convinced me to check out of the motel I'd called home for the last month. It made sense. If I was working in Fletcher Canyon with Mom, why commute from Hollywood? Mom reasoned I'd be better off just moving back home with her. It made sense financially, but I didn't know if it was the right move for me. It's one thing to have to start over again. It's another, more depressing thing, to be a grown woman moving back home to be taken care of by her mother.

"Give me a second, kid," Mom said as she dug around in her purse.

"No problem," I said. An upside to being lost in life is there's no reason to be in a hurry.

I looked out at Main Street, a two-lane, tree-lined road at the foot of the mountain. It was only six blocks, but all the residents called it "downtown". The barber shop at the far end of the street had been there for over one hundred years. There'd been renovations to the inside, but the barber pole out front remained unchanged. A bus made up to look like a red-and-white trolley ran up and down the street and around to the Civic Center that housed the court-house, post office, and the sheriff's substation we shared with the neighboring town.

Main Street housed the local eateries, a laundro-mat/dry cleaner, a bookstore, a pharmacy, a vegetable market, and a few other stores I didn't recognize. I'd thought this little town was boring as a kid, but now it felt quaint and peaceful.

"All set," Mom said, her fists full of change as she stepped out of the car. I followed. For a quick second, I'd worried about leaving my stuff in the car, but then I remembered this was Fletcher Canyon, not Hollywood.

I waited as Mom pumped change into the meter. A lot of change.

"Mom, there's a two-hour limit," I said.

Mom laughed. "Not here," she said. "Next time you can park in the employee parking behind the restaurant."

"Why didn't we do that this time?" I asked.

Mom did the thing she does when she doesn't want to answer my question. She acts like she didn't hear me and changes the subject. "Look there's, Todd!" Mom said, pointing to the publisher and editor of The Fletcher Canyon Weekly headed our way. "Hi, Todd!" Mom said walking over to him.

"Hi, Jo!" he said. "Any news?"

"My daughter is back in town," Mom said. "She's moved back to help me with the business."

"Well, let me know if you want to take out an ad in the paper," he said and then turned to me. "Welcome back, and," he paused, "I'm sorry to hear about your husband."

"Uh thanks," I said, but before I could ask what he meant about my husband, Mom pulled me down the street.

"Let's go," she said. "I texted Wenling we were coming ages ago."

Wenling owned The Lucky Dragon Restaurant and had been Mom's best friend for years. They'd met when they were both featured extras on a major television show whose name I'm not sure I can legally mention. Let's just say that Los Angeles casting directors in the late seventies and early eighties needed any Asian women, even if they were Chinese or Filipino, to play war-torn Koreans.

My dad was a Teamster for Local 399 and drove for that same TV show for all eleven seasons. He was the one who convinced Mom to go on the casting call. Mom will still get the occasional call for commercials and modeling work. Nobody ever would guess it, because she has such a happy expression all the time, but Mom's "sad face" is epic. When they need an older woman to look sad in some kind of environment brochure or war show, Mom's phone will ring.

We got about three yards before Mom ran into someone else she knew. Mom stopped to introduce me once again, saying I'd moved home to help her (a face-saving gesture I appreciated). Mom talked some more. I stood by and waited.

Mom finished talking to the lady whose name I'd already forgotten, because Mom was shouting across the street to another woman she knew. "Hi, Edna!" Mom said, waving to the woman on the other side of the street. The woman waved back, and Mom yelled. "This is my daughter. She just moved back."

Edna smiled and waved to me. I returned the wave, but even as Edna went into the pharmacy, Mom spotted yet another person down the street that she knew. Mom made a motion to me. More smiles and waving. I started to think I knew the reason Mom wanted to park on Main Street even if it meant paying for the meter. Nobody would see us if we parked in the alley and came through the kitchen door.

We continued down the street and passed the ice cream shop next door to The Lucky Dragon. I gazed in through the glass storefront at its black and white checkered tiles and clean white soda fountain counter with shiny chrome edges. It looked like something out of a Frank Capra movie. I'd definitely missed this ice cream place. My folks moved to Fletcher Canyon even though it was a little out of the way, because Mom and Dad weren't "Hollywood types." They liked living in a small town.

We finally reached the Lucky Dragon. Mom opened the door. The gust of air conditioning and the sound of the running water on the small fountain next to the hostess station greeted us. My mind flooded with memories. We ate here every Saturday night when I was a kid. The restaurant had two sections. The left side, which was closed during the slow times like now, and one to the right that remained open all the time. Mom headed straight to the closed section and waved to Wenling seated in the back booth. Wenling waved back, but once she spotted me she jumped up for a hug. "Christy! You came. I was worried when it took so long."

Wenling is even shorter than my Mom, who is only 5'1". Like Mom, she has dyed black hair, but Wenling's was cut into a short bob, whereas Mom's hair was long and pulled back in a high pony tail. I hugged Wenling carefully, to go easy on her small frame. Sometimes I worried if I hugged her too hard, I'd break her. Mom is small framed as well, but feels less fragile when we hug.

"You look great!" Wenling said as we walked back to the booth. "So healthy!"

For the record, I knew I looked awful, and I secretly believe Wenling has the words "hefty" and "healthy" mixed up. I'm pretty sure I've heard her the phrase "healthy trash bags" before. I've always been a bigger girl. Mom is great about it. She says it's very trendy to be a "big girl" these days. I guess I'm getting better with it. I figure I got my "healthy" shape from my father's genes, and, of course, food.

"What do you want to eat?" Wenling asked.

"Broccoli chicken," I said. After a month of Pete's Burger, I craved vegetables big time.

"I'm not too hungry," Mom said, "But maybe some rice and a side of mixed vegetables I'll share with the kid," Mom added. Wenling smiled and left to put in our order.

I looked at Mom with surprise. "How did you know I was craving vegetables?" I'd developed a mean junk food habit in the last two years as my marriage fell apart.

Mom laughed. "You've always like vegetables when you were a kid. You'd eat them without even thinking about it."

"Mom, I ate everything," I said.

"You've eaten greasy burger for a month. I'm surprised you can even poop with that kind of diet."

I had no comment.

Wenling came back from the kitchen and cleared the

portable television off the table. Mom hung out at the restaurant most afternoons with Wenling watching crime shows and folding wontons. Mom used the restaurant's kitchen for her catering in exchange for helping out and making desserts. The health department only allows certain foods to be homemade, so having an inspected "commercial kitchen" made things easy for Mom.

It was a little after four in the afternoon, a slow time for the restaurant. The lunch special ended at four, and the dinner rush didn't start until six. That's if things hadn't changed much since I'd last visited.

"So you're going to help out your Mom," Wenling said as we sat down. She'd brought me a diet soda even though I hadn't asked. I smiled. It was just what I wanted. I'd forgotten how nice it was to be around people who'd known me for most of my life. "Jennifer runs the restaurant for me now. Maybe one day you'll take over the catering now that you've moved back."

I hadn't thought of this as a career move, and I wasn't sure what Wenling meant by "moved back." I'd decided to stay at Mom's for a few days, but I wasn't sure that I would stay any longer. I might get a part time job just to have a little more money to afford an apartment sooner.

The bell over the front door jingled, interrupting my thoughts.

"Tita Jo! Are you here?" my cousin Celia called out.

"Over here," Mom called back.

"We don't have time to play Marco Polo!" an angry, male voice croaked.

Celia peeked around the corner. "It's okay, sir. We found them." Celia was thin, but tall. She had a job as a nurse for a prominent home healthcare agency. Being in the medical profession is a big deal in Filipino culture. When I'd scored high in math and science testing in middle school Mom had big hopes for my future as a doctor. Let's just say she's had to scale back her expectations.

"It's not like you'll let me eat this food today, anyway," the man growled back.

"You'll have a special treat for your birthday," Celia assured her charge.

"It better be real food. Not that low sodium stuff," the man barked back.

Celia ignored him. "Guess whose birthday is this Saturday?" Celia said to us.

"Happy birthday, Harold," Mom said to the older man. Wenling and I said happy birthday, too.

"Don't kiss up now. I'm not going to bother updating the will and you're not in it," he said, and then turned to back to Celia. "Tell the one that makes the cake that I want that cake. It's got to be the one from Christmas, or I don't want a dang party or any of it."

"Sir would like to have you cater his birthday party, Tita Jo. We'll need your mango cake for 25 guests,"

"The one you gave me a slice of at Christmas! It was orange colored," he said.

"I remember," Mom said.

"And of course we'll have Chinese food. I wrote down Ma'am Margaret's number. She's organizing the party." She handed Mom the paper with the phone number of Harold Sanders' daughter Margaret. Underneath, in huge letters, were the words "low sodium menu." Celia added with a quick wink, "Make the Chinese food like you normally would."

"No low salt! And use that MSG if it makes it taste good," Harold interrupted.

"Yes," Celia said with a smile, while shaking her head like don't do what I'm saying. "No low salt and lots of tasty MSG."

"And a full bar," he said. "Those people will need a stiff drink if they are forced to talk with my nut job of a daughter."

"The party is this Saturday," Celia said. "I know it's last minute. Ma'am Margaret said she'd pay the rush fee. You can do it, right?"

"No problem," Mom said, but I caught a doubtful look from Wenling that I couldn't decipher.

The bell over the front door jingled again. "Yoo-hoo!" a female voice called out. "Did I just see you, Celia?"

Celia rolled her eyes. I'd never seen her do that before. "Yes, Jess. I'm here."

A woman with black hair, overdrawn eyebrows, and bright red lipstick approached us. "There you are. I just came to ask what you're going to bring to the church's charity auction. I'm donating a week at our Colorado cabin with airfare for two. Naturally, you can't afford to do that, but perhaps maybe you can put together something."

Jess's haughty demeanor caught me off guard. I admired that Celia kept her cool.

"I'll let you know at church on Sunday. I haven't had a chance to work it out just yet," Celia said. "Us career women," she said pointing to Mom, Wenling, and me, "have so much to balance. I'm not sure you'd understand."

Wenling and I traded glances. What a burn!

"How quaint!" Jess replied. (Who says that any more?) "I'll tell the committee to expect your answer this Sunday," she continued and then turned and left without saying goodbye.

Mr. Sanders looked at his watch and tugged at Celia's arm. "We're late. We need to get to the pharmacy."

"Ma'am Margaret said to call and set up a time to go

over the details on Thursday," Celia said as she waved goodbye and headed to the door.

"Maybe we'll run into someone we can invite to the party," Celia said, smiling at the man.

"All my friends are dead," he barked back as they left.

"Isn't it great, we have a gig! I told you business is booming," Mom said to me. "Let's eat our lunch, it's getting cold."

Wenling's expression told me something wasn't as "great" as Mom said it was. "But what about the van? Clifford and his family are moving on Friday. How can you cater without a van? You don't even drive," Wenling said to Mom.

Mom did that thing where she ignored the question and changed the subject. "We need to go shopping early tomorrow and pick up stuff for the party," she said. Perhaps Mom did need a little help–especially with this van situation.

Although our new van had air conditioning, I realized how smart Mom was to keep our shirts hanging. If I'd worn my tuxedo shirt during the drive, it would've been soaked. Driving up to the top of the ever-winding Marple Drive, I was wetter than a baby diaper, and my muscles were tighter than my bank account.

Mom was uncharacteristically quiet as I negotiated the road.

I'd traded in my Honda as a down payment on our new van. Now, we just needed to make sure we booked enough gigs to make the payments. But as worried as I was about our ability to afford the van, my more immediate concern was not killing us both driving this giant vehicle.

Having driven an automatic, compact car my entire life, I'd never realized how thin and twisty a mountain road can be, and how death defying going uphill with a manual transmission might feel. I pulled onto the private road, punched in the gate code, and found the driveway of what I hoped was the house of our eighty-five-year old "birthday boy's" party. Mom sprang out of the van, eager to be on solid earth, and headed for the front door. I took a deep breath, triple-checked the van was in park and made sure the emergency brake was engaged. Then I slid out of the van and jogged up the walk to catch up with Mom.

"Every day an adventure, kid," Mom said when I got to her side. She'd snapped back to her usual happy self. Mom's ability to move on was the polar opposite of mine. I was kind of a dweller, but I'm working on it. We strode up the long front walk to ring the doorbell. Before we even got to the door Celia came out.

"We're here!" I said to my cousin. It felt like an achievement that required an announcement. Celia did not seem impressed.

Before she could speak, I heard yelling, and from the look on Mom's face, she did, too. Celia closed the door behind her.

"Um," Celia said. "We might want to wait before you bring the stuff inside."

Mom gave Celia a questioning look. "Did the tables and chairs not arrive? Is that why they're yelling?" Mom asked.

Celia walked a few steps further from the house. "No, they came, but you might have to wait, because there might not be a party."

"No party!" Mom exclaimed.

Celia put her finger to her lips to indicate we should be quiet. "Ma'am Margaret and Sir are fighting. He said 'no party'."

"He did not," Mom argued as if she knew.

Celia nodded with a grave face that indeed he had. "Come around the side door and wait inside," Celia said as she led us across the lawn.

"We'll wait there for the air to clear so they can change their mind," I said.

"No, but we'll hear the fight better inside," Celia answered.

———

"NICE KITCHEN," MOM SAID AS WE ENTERED through the side door.

"It's okay," Celia said, pretending it was no big deal. She'd been like that ever since she'd came to the United States from the Philippines. "I have another family that has a kitchen twice the size and a full-time chef."

Mom made a face that said she was impressed, but I found it annoying. My mother's family had some very lean years after the death of my grandmother. They'd been well off before then, and Celia had always acted as if she'd grown up rich. I knew better.

The arguing continued in another part of the house, but we couldn't make out what they were saying. A few minutes later, the shouts grew louder. I felt uncomfortable eavesdropping, but Mom and Celia were totally absorbed. They listened as if it was a soap opera.

"You're a thief and you know it!" Harold yelled.

"That's ridiculous! You probably forgot that you wrote those checks, just like you forgot where you left Mother's antique pearl necklace!" Margaret responded.

"What checks?" Mom whispered to Celia.

"Sir Harold went to his checkbook this morning to pay for the party, and he noticed that there were other checks that he didn't write in the book. He thinks Ma'am Margaret forged the missing checks."

"What about the necklace?" Mom asked.

Celia shrugged her shoulders, and we all went back to listening to the father and daughter argue.

"We can talk about this later," Margaret said. "We have to get ready for the party."

"I told you. There isn't going to be a darn party! I didn't want to host your freak show in the first place!" He yelled back.

"Mom," I whispered, my gut sinking knowing that our first gig together might end in disaster. "When you finalized the agreement with Margaret on

Thursday, did you mention a fee or policy regarding last-minute cancellations?"

Mom looked back at me, her eyes wide with a combination of surprise and remorse. "No."

The three of us remained quiet as we leaned against the granite countertop.

Celia broke the silence. "The party would've been weird anyway." She turned to Mom. "Aunt Jo, can we eat some of the food while we wait for the fight to end? I'm hungry."

I was hungry, too, and I loved Mom's mango cake. Even snobby Celia knew it was the best.

"By the way," Celia said, turning to me. "Sorry to hear about your husband."

I wanted to ask her what she meant by that, but a slamming door distracted me.

Mom, Celia, and I traded glances. We all heard the stomping of feet getting closer. An older, trim woman in her sixties with long, hippy-like gray-streaked hair stormed into the kitchen. It surprised me she could stomp that loud considering her tall, graceful frame.

"Who are these people, Celia?" she asked.

"Ma'am Margaret. This is my aunt and her daughter for the catering."

"Oh." The woman's anger subsided, and then she burst into tears. "I'm sorry I didn't recognize you," she said to Mom. "So sorry, but there isn't going to be a party. And my dreams for my new business will be dashed."

Mom shot me a questioning look, and I gave a slight shrug to let her know that I didn't know either. We both assumed the older man's birthday was the sole reason for the party.

"Maybe we can have the party without him?" Celia suggested.

"He has the checkbook. He'd never pay for it now," Margaret wept. "And I took so much time getting ready for the party."

My hopes for a cancellation fee sank.

"It's okay," Mom said, walking up to Margaret and patting her on the back. "I'll talk to him, and we'll have a party."

The woman sniffed. "Really?"

I had the same thought. Why was Mom so sure she could convince the grouchy man to have a party?

Mom assured Margaret that she would take care of it, and Margaret believed her. "My daughter," Mom said, "will help with the decorations, setting up the bar, and then show her where to start loading in the food."

Margaret smiled. "That sounds great. Thank you."

"Where do I go to talk to your father?"

"Sir's in his study," Celia said. "Up the stairs at the back of the kitchen, down the hall, and to your right."

Mom left. Margaret turned to us. "Now that that's settled, let's get ready for the party!"

I didn't think it was settled at all, but I didn't have time to dwell on that, as Margaret led us into the living room that she'd cleared and "decorated" for the party.

I blinked three times, unsure of what I saw.

"I told you the party was going to be weird," Celia said. Weird didn't quite cover it for me.

————

Mom somehow convinced Harold to agree to go on with the party plans. He even helped us move the catering van to the side entrance near the kitchen. And by helped, I mean he hopped into the van, popped it into reverse, and expertly backed it right up to the door in five minutes.

Celia, Mom and I took a quick break and watched him. Mom drank coffee, and I had my second diet soda of the day.

"Thank you!" I said to him as we walked into the kitchen.

"Women can't drive. It's to be expected," he said.

"Hey, can I have some of that?" he asked pointed to my soda.

"I can do better than that, I'll get you your own can," I said.

Harold Sanders almost smiled, but thought better of it. I handed him a glass of ice and a can. Celia didn't look too happy. I guess it was the sodium. Harold saw Celia's disapproving expression, clutched the glass to his chest, muttered a few choice words, and left.

Mom stayed in the kitchen and rushed to prepare the trays for the hors d'oeuvres. Celia and I set up the chafing dishes on the buffet table in the living room. Margaret had had the company who brought the table and chairs move the larger sofas into another room for the party. We lit the burners and covered the trays to keep the food warm until meal time. The food would be served after the presents were unwrapped. I set up the bar for Mom and then dashed back into the kitchen.

With the drama delaying our prep time, Mom and I changed into our tuxedo shirts in the kitchen and snapped on our pre-tied bow ties just as the doorbell rang. Mom rushed to the living room to get behind the bar while I grabbed a serving tray.

"Aye!" I heard her scream, and I remembered that Mom hadn't seen Margaret's special art / new business venture.

I entered the living room just as Margaret was showing off the taxidermic raccoon with a balloon tied around his paw to the first stunned guest.

"Bandit was a beloved backyard pet," she said, "and now he can be enjoyed by generations." She went on to introduce Hootie, the owl with festive streamers tied around his neck, and finally, Duke, a Great Dane sporting a party hat.

I looked over to Mom, who'd scooted around the edge of the living room to get behind the bar. She widened her eyes in a way they let me know that Mom would not be a future customer of "Margaret's Memorial Taxidermy." Margaret assured her guest, an older man, that taxidermy would be the next "big thing".

The man seemed disturbed. I offered him some crab wanton, but he passed me by and headed straight for Mom at the bar.

Three more guest filtered in, but the large, ornate living room looked very empty. Celia helped herself to some crab rangoon. I shot her a look. "I'm a guest," she said. "Sir invited me." I decided it was better for her to be a guest than the help at this stage of the party.

Celia turned up her nose, sauntered over to the stuffed animals, and pretended to be fascinated with the taxidermy, even though I knew she didn't like them. "So lifelike," she said to Margaret, who ate up the compliment. The three guests, who I'd later find out were the Turner family, didn't do a great job of hiding the horror at the stuffed partygoers.

"We won't be able to stay long," Oscar Turner said. "We have to be up early." His wife and son nodded in agreement and headed to Mom at the bar.

A man I hadn't seen before came down the main stairwell near the front door and jumped into the conversation. "Getting involved with Dad in business is likely to land you in jail."

"George, if you're going to be like that, you shouldn't have even come," Margaret said, her voice a little too loud. George ignored her and headed to the bar. I got the vibe that this wasn't his first drink of the day.

Knowing that he was Margaret's brother, I was able to see the family resemblance. They both were tall, Margaret must've been 5′10″ and her brother well over six feet. He was balding, but what was left was also gray-streaked, but where Margaret was fit with a healthy glow, her brother had that puffy, boozy look complete with a red nose and cheeks. In that moment, I was glad I was more of an eater than a drinker. Sure, I had a puffy face, but my nose was less Rudolph-like.

The doorbell quashed the budding family argument. Margaret was excited to greet the new arrival, a very beautiful older lady with perfectly coiffed hair. It took me a moment to recognize her from Main Street earlier in the week.

"Edna!" the first houseguest called out.

"Charles! I didn't know you'd be here," she said.

"I got in town yesterday. First thing I did was visit my best buddy and ask him about you," Charles said. They made small talk, and Edna escaped to the ladies room. I got the vibe this party might be in a death spiral.

Margaret decided that the party needed some music and put on the Bee Gees, and then boogied over to me to ask me to fetch the guest of honor.

I'd say the rest was a blur, but that's not how my weird brain works.

A MEMORY FOR MURDER

M om, Celia, and I waited by the food on the far side of the living room. The guests sat on folding chairs we'd placed on the other side. We were told not to leave. My gaze drifted to Bandit, the stuffed raccoon with the balloon. The EMT had confirmed that Mr. Sanders hadn't made it, and a small part of me worried that Margaret might try to memorialize Harold in a Bandit-like fashion so he could "be enjoyed by generations."

"I think he was murdered," Mom whispered to me.

At first I thought she was talking about the raccoon, and my brain spat out Margaret as the prime suspect. Thank goodness I caught on a second later.

"Harold was 85 years old," I whispered back. "It's probably natural causes." But details from the den peppered my brain: the pills on the floor, the knocked over furniture, the scattered papers, the open checkbook.

"They'll think it's me," Celia butted in, also keeping her voice low.

"They won't," I said, annoyed that Celia's need to be special even encompassed being a murder suspect.

"They always say, the butler did it," she said.

"You're a home healthcare worker!" I said. "If anyone is the butler here, it's me. I'm the one serving the food."

We stood and scowled at one another in silence until the doorbell rang. Margaret answered the door. A handsome man just under six feet tall, with salt and pepper hair and blue eyes, entered the house and spoke to Margaret. He looked like a mix between Henry Rollins and a young Ed Harris with more hair.

After a few minutes of talking with the hostess, fantasy Henry/Ed turned away from Margaret and glanced around the room. His eyes locked on mine. My heart did that flutter thing I'd imagined only happened in movies. I could almost hear the music swell.

He turned back to Margaret and said, "Is she the one who found the dead body?"

Rats. I thought we had "a thing" there.

Margaret must've answered him, because he crossed the room and approached me.

"Ma'am," he said.

Ma'am! I was at the ma'am stage in my life. We definitely did not have "a thing" at all. Unless it was a ma'am thing, in which case I'd rather have no thing. Well, nothing is what I had.

"Her name is Christy," Mom chimed in. "She's my beautiful, single daughter."

My face heated with embarrassment. Mom hit that word "single" hard and loud. The man smiled.

"I'm Detective D.C. Cooper, and I need to ask you some questions." He reached for his pad and pen.

I nodded, unable to talk. My eyes had followed his

hands to his shirt pocket and got distracted by how broad his chest and shoulders were. My traumatized brain remembered every inch of him, and for once, I was glad.

"Christy, is it?" he said clearing his throat.

My eyes shot back up to his, but it was too late. I was totally busted on checking him out.

Annoying Celia let out an "ooh," like kids do during the kissing parts of a movie to add to my humiliation. A part of me wished I'd crashed our catering van on the way over.

D. C. Cooper shook his head, looked down at his pad, and smiled. "Do you remember what time you found the body?"

"The clock on the study wall read 4:22 when I looked up at it. It couldn't have been more than a minute or two before that when I saw the body."

The detective looked up at me. "4:22?"

"According to the clock in that room, but after the ambulance arrived, the den clock read 4:52, and when I came downstairs the grandfather clock over there," I pointed to the antique clock against the wall not too far from us, "read 4:45. So one of those clocks has to be wrong, but I'm sure you can check by your official detective time and figure it out from there," I said, and then took a huge gulp of air.

"You remember a lot of details," he said, but his voice sounded more like a question.

"She remembers all the details," Mom said.

"You have one of those photographic memories?" he asked.

"Something like that," I answered. "Except it only kicks in when really bad things happen."

"I see. And 'really bad things' happen around you so often, you've recognized a pattern in your memory. Is that right?" he asked.

I liked that the man was smart and a good listener, but I didn't like the part where he was suspicious of me. I was starting to think by the tone and veracity of his questions that this might turn into one of those "the butler did it" scenarios. Heck, he had such a commanding presence, I almost thought I had done it.

———

I peeked out the kitchen door and watched as Detective Cooper questioned the other guests. Mom joined me in my snooping. He didn't spend nearly as long with each of the guests as he did me. He and Mom seemed to get along like a house on fire during their questioning. Celia's interview went a tad better than mine, but not by much.

The Thomas's looked like they were off the hook. They'd never been to this house before and had only just met Margaret at her yoga class earlier that week. DC interviewed Edna next. Charles, the first guest, stood close by. It looked like he wanted to protect her and console her, an old-school gentlemanly move. I wished my ex had been like that.

"So how did you know the deceased?" Detective Cooper asked Edna.

"We'd gone to high school together. Charles did, too," Edna said, motioning at her protector. "Then, I went to boarding school, graduated, got married, children, grandchildren." She paused to take a breath, her face sad for a moment. "I moved back about a year ago after my husband died. My sister had been living in our parents' house after they passed, but she moved to Florida to be closer to her grandkids, so I moved here. Upstate New York gets so cold in winter, and I didn't have anyone to shovel the snow anymore."

She paused again. Charles patted her on the shoulder. Edna gave a weak smile and continued, "I'd see Harold around town. At the pharmacy and what not. We'd have coffee sometimes when his aid, Celia, would have to run other errands."

"And what time did you arrive at the party?" he asked.

"I imagine not long after four. Maybe ten minutes late. I think I was the last to arrive," she said.

"That's right," Charles reassured.

"You don't think this was anything other than natural causes, do you?" Edna asked the detective.

"He looked healthy as a horse when I saw him yesterday," Charles said. "But at our age, there's no way to know for sure."

The three of them spoke for a few minutes longer. I couldn't make out exactly what they said, but it didn't seem important. Detective Cooper had tucked his pad back into his pocket. The detective turned back to Margaret. "I understand your brother was here. I'll need to talk to him."

"He's upstairs," Margaret said. "Father's passing hit him pretty hard."

Mom and I traded a look. It was more like the booze hit him pretty hard. The guests didn't seem to buy Margaret's version of events either. Margaret and Detective Cooper headed upstairs to talk to George Sanders.

Mom and I went back to our work. We'd hauled the trays into the kitchen to pack the uneaten food. Margaret didn't want to keep the dinner at first, but Mom offered to make "a few plates" for the guests and Margaret to have for later. Mom cut and wrapped several slices of cake, careful not to cut off any of Harold's name into the pieces. She said it might be "too depressing" and wrapped those as well. I wouldn't mind taking the depressing Harold piece home.

Celia continued to chow down on the leftovers. She even asked if it was okay if she took some home for her family. Celia was happily married to a doctor and had two perfect children. She ate like a piranha and never gained any weight. Life didn't have to be fair, but I always wanted it to be unfair in my favor.

A half hour went by, and we heard footsteps on the main stairwell. Mom handed me a paper plate wrapped in tinfoil and elbowed me. "This is for DC," Mom said like they were old friends. Mom's chat with the officer had a lot more laughing than mine. Mom got along with everyone. "Come on. Go out there before he leaves."

"He's working, Mom. Besides, I don't think he can have food on the job."

"It's wrapped up for later," Mom said, "and police can eat on the job. How else would those cop-eating-donut jokes make sense?"

She had a point, but I wasn't going to bring him a plate of food.

"Now that I think about it," Mom said half to herself, "I should give him a big slice of cake."

Mom rushed over to the counter and snagged one slice she'd pre-wrapped, but then thought better of it. "He can have the piece with Harold's name. It's the biggest, and he's used to dead people," Mom said and then rushed back to the kitchen door and poked her head out. I spied over her shoulder. He was talking to Margaret, and it looked like he was getting ready to leave.

"Hurry!" Mom said, but I shook my head no.

"Someone will be in touch as to when the coroner's office will release the body," he said to Margaret.

Mom elbowed me again, but I wouldn't budge, so she barged out the door. "DC, wait!" Mom said. He stopped. "I wrapped some food for you."

He gave Mom a friendly smile and tried to decline her offer. I scooted out of the kitchen and came closer. It looked like Mom would win the argument, and he didn't seem to mind. Mom whispered something in his ear, and then he laughed and blushed. Their whispering drew me closer.

"That is something to consider, Jo," he said.

Jo! I got ma'am-ed, and he called Mom Jo. He turned to me with those blue eyes. A zing of excitement pulsed through me, and then he said, "And as for you. I think it's best you don't leave town."

Mom laughed and gave him a playful nudge as he left, but I wasn't sure he was joking. The guests filtered out of the party. Mom gave each of them food for later, and Margaret insisted they take their gifts back. It was like we'd all lost as contestants on the most depressing game show, and they were reluctantly taking their "parting gifts."

The doorbell rang. Margaret said, "Oh no. That might be a late arriving guest."

"Would you like me to tell them?" Mom asked.

"Would you?" Margaret said. "I'm going to check on my brother."

"I'll take care of it," Mom said, going to the door. Margaret headed up the main staircase. Mom motioned to me. "Get more food," she said.

I dashed to the kitchen and fetched a few of the wrapped dinner plates and slices of cake. My mind filled with dread. How would we break the news to a stranger? When I returned to the living room Mom was talking to an older couple at the door. "He's dead, so there's no party," Mom said plainly. "So sorry. Please take dinner and cake. I'm sure you can get a refund for the gifts."

I guess that problem was solved.

I handed the couple their two dinners and slices of cake. "It looks delicious," the woman said.

"Our card is in there if you need any catering," Mom said.

"What kind of cake is it?" the man asked.

"Mango cake," Mom said.

The gentleman asked for another slice of cake, and I gave it to him. They asked us to pass their condolences onto the family and left. I was impressed at how well they took the news.

The doorbell rang a few more times over the course of the next hour. Margaret stayed upstairs, content to let Mom tell the guests that Harold was dead and the party was canceled. Somehow this odd exchange was less awkward than the actual party. Man, that was a bad party.

After no new guests arrived for a good half hour, Margaret came downstairs to thank us for all of our help. I'd taken down all the party decorations in between the late-arriving guests. The only remaining decorations were those left on Margaret's memorialized pets.

I looked over at the taxidermic animals. They were dressed for a party that never came to pass. It was then I noticed for the first time a stuffed tuxedo cat on the table next to the raccoon. He looked so lifelike, I stepped closer to get a better look. Perhaps Margaret's business idea wasn't so odd.

I leaned forward. His fur looked so soft and shiny I wanted to pet him. "I didn't catch this one's name," I said to Margaret.

"Which one?" she asked.

"This tuxedo cat," I said pointing to the black and white kitty. I turned away to face Margaret for a moment and a flash of fur flew at me. Before my brain could register what happened, the cat leapt to life and attacked my hand with a loud meow. I shrieked. The frightened cat bolted across the living room and out an open window.

Mom laughed and laughed. Margaret and Celia joined her.

I tried to get my heart to start again.

I f I thought driving down the windy road in the daylight was terrifying, doing so at night became an out-of-body experience. I was so frightened that I swore I could hear a ghost howling in the distance. My brain figured it was the ghost of van drivers past, who'd come to warn me of our cliff-diving future.

Mom and I remained silent. I wasn't sure if it was my driving or the murder, but when we reached the bottom of the hill, it hit me.

"Mom, we forgot to get paid!"

Mom laughed. "I got the check from Harold before. He was such a nice guy. It's a shame his son murdered him."

"He wasn't that nice," I said to Mom.

"You haven't seen the check," Mom answered.

I smiled, not just because we got paid, but also because we were back on flat ground, and there were only three right turns until home. Mom's murder comment registered in my brain, but I was too busy trying to downshift to make my turn. I'd taken a turn in fourth earlier, and the van had almost tipped over on its side. Five quiet, stress-focused minutes later, I pulled into our driveway.

Even though it would've been easier for us if I backed into the driveway, I didn't want to risk crashing into the house. So, I pulled in front-first. Mom said nothing. Luckily our house has a large driveway at far end of a cul-de-sac. We only have two neighbors, and since our house is on a little over an acre, they couldn't see my horrible driving.

"Why do you think the son murdered him? If anyone, wouldn't you think it was Margaret?"

"Margaret's too obvious. It's the son. I overheard when I was bartending that he served two years in prison for accounting fraud. He blames his father."

I didn't want to believe that the nice man we'd met had been murdered. "We don't even really know if he was murdered. The man was eighty-five years old. It's likely to be natural causes."

"But didn't you say you saw all the pills scattered on the floor?" Mom asked. "And you told DC that the furniture was knocked over."

"That's true," I said, and made sure I engaged the emergency brake before sliding out of the van. The stress of the day exhausted me. Mom met me at the back of the van as I unlocked the double doors. "Maybe he knocked over his medication reaching for the phone while having a heart attack," I said.

"Tell me about the position of the phone. Wasn't it closer to his body than the lamp and the chair?"

"Yeah," I said remembering how the phone was closer and none of the items on the desk were disturbed. "He could have fallen and knocked them over," I suggested, but I didn't quite believe my own theory.

"What else was near the phone?" Mom asked as we pulled the collapsible rolling cart out of the van and unfolded the legs.

"His checkbook, the empty can of diet soda." I said.

"Where was the glass you gave him?" Mom asked.

"On the floor, a few feet from the body. It looked like it rolled away, but that doesn't prove murder. Does it?" I asked.

"Prove murder? No, but I think he died taking those pills," Mom said.

What Mom said made sense, but I didn't think it was the only explanation. We unloaded the equipment we kept in the garage onto the cart, along with the leftover food we'd no doubt be eating for days. The rest of the stuff Mom told me we'd leave in the van to bring back to the restaurant. We worked quickly. It wasn't yet eight at night, but I was exhausted.

"By the way, Mom. How did you get Harold Sanders to agree to the party?" I asked as I reached for one of the large pans filled with broccoli beef.

Mom didn't answer. Something in the van distracted her. I turned and bent down to see what she was looking at. I didn't see anything, so I kept moving toward the van. Suddenly a loud shrieking noise pierced my ears, and two seconds later something leapt out at me! I screamed and jumped, spilling broccoli beef all over myself and the van.

———

WENLING AND MOM COVERED THEIR MOUTHS AS they laughed. "It was so funny!" Mom choked out. "The cat shrieked, and then Christy made a noise worse than cat." Mom's accent, and her dropping of prepositions becomes more pronounced when she talks to Wenling.

It was a slow day at the restaurant. We'd allegedly come for lunch, but it was almost four in the afternoon, and we were just drinking coffee. Well, Wenling was drinking tea. Everyone kept stopping by to hear about "the murder," and no one wanted to listen to my more boring theory that Harold Sanders died of natural causes. Mom held back on her theory about the brother and most of the "good stuff" just in case my boring theory held true. She spent most of her time talking about how that tuxedo cat had enjoyed scaring me so much at the Sanders' house that he stowed away in the van to frighten me again.

"We should go back and check with Margaret in case she knows who the owner is," I said.

"I think we should keep him," Mom said.

"He got beef broccoli all over our van," I said.

Mom and Wenling laughed some more. "She has good taste in food!" Mom said.

"It's a he," I said trying not to laugh, but the whole thing was just so stupid.

Before I could get up to refill my coffee, Jennifer returned from running her afternoon errands. "Did you hear the news?"

The urgency in her voice gripped our attention, and our eyes snapped to Jennifer. It was so odd to see her all grown up. I used to babysit her, and now she had a child of her own.

"What happened?" Wenling asked.

"Celia got arrested for murder!" Jennifer answered.

All three of us were stunned.

"When?" I asked.

Jennifer shook her head, "Sometime this afternoon."

"Are you sure?" I asked.

"I was at the dry cleaners, and Mrs. Lim told me," Jennifer answered.

"Aye! It must be true," Mom said. "Her son works as a court reporter."

"Why?" I asked.

Wenling jumped in. "The courthouse is right across the street from the police."

Jennifer nodded. "Mrs. Lim's son saw her being taken out of the police car when he was taking a smoke break."

"He should stop smoking. He's so good looking. It will ruin his skin," Mom said.

Wenling agreed.

"They could have been just taking her there for questioning," I said.

"Mrs. Lim said her son told her that Celia was in handcuffs," Jennifer said.

"Then it's true," Wenling said, and Mom agreed.

"This has to be a mistake," I said. Sure, I didn't always

like my cousin, but she couldn't be a murderer. She just couldn't be.

"It's such a shame," Mom said.

"I know," I said. "Celia doesn't deserve to be arrested."

"No, she doesn't," Mom said and then added, "and I don't think we'll be catering the funeral, even though I promised Miss Sanders a good price."

———

THE NEXT DAY I WOKE UP IN THE ROOM I'D shared with my older sister growing up. Except, instead of listening to the radio and trying to figure out a way to get my sister to let me hang out with her cool friends, my thoughts were consumed by the murder. Celia hadn't done it. She'd been at the party the whole time. Even when I came downstairs after calling 911, she was still in the living room where I'd last seen her.

I squinted at the radio alarm clock on my bedside table before giving up and grabbing my glasses off the nightstand. It was almost ten in the morning. That old alarm clock used to be in my parents' room. I smiled as I remembered sitting on their bed while they got ready for work. I missed the smell of Dad's aftershave. Celia had comforted me so much after he died. She understood what I was going through, having lost her Mom. There's no way Celia would ever kill anyone.

The more I thought about it, the more I was sure that Mom was right. It had to have been the son, George. On Harold Sanders' desk along with the checkbook, I remember seeing a business proposal for Margaret's Memorial keepsakes. Between George's hatred of his father over going to jail, and the jealous way he reacted to the idea that Harold Sanders might fund Margaret's new business, George probably snapped. We needed to talk some sense into DC Cooper.

My thoughts were interrupted by the smell of coffee coming from the kitchen. I'd inherited my coffee addiction from my mother. Of course, both of us had recently switched to half-caff. Between my divorce and the dozen or so cups I drank a day, I'd developed heart palpitations and an eye twitch. Mom switched in solidarity.

I resolved to grab a cup of coffee before getting dressed and heading down to the police station. DC

Cooper would have to listen. I stumbled to the kitchen without bothering to brush my hair or my teeth. Everything could wait until after coffee. Mom made the best cup of coffee. I don't know how she did it. She used the same cheap coffee from the store and a normal coffee pot, but it just tasted better. Maybe the tap water in Fletcher Grove was better than the water in Hollywood, I didn't know.

I entered the kitchen and found Mom at her usual place at the kitchen table reading the paper. She'd always skipped over the news and checked the obituaries to see who was dead. I didn't see why she had to check today. We already knew. I'm not a big talker before my coffee, so we enjoyed a comfortable silence. Two sips into my morning joe, the doorbell rang.

Mom jumped up to get it. I assumed she was waiting for a package. She liked to order weird stuff off the television all the time, and I wasn't dressed suitably enough to meet the delivery man. I sipped my coffee and woke up a little, but I wasn't at the point of being a fully coherent human yet. That wouldn't happen until my second cup. A male voice boomed at the front door.

"Have a seat. I'll go get her," I heard Mom say and seconds later she entered the kitchen. "Kid, he's here."

"Who's here?"

"DC. He needs to ask us some questions."

Absolute. Total. Panic.

"Mom, I'm not dressed yet."

"Well then get dressed," she said.

"Is he in the living room?"

"Yes, hurry up."

"How am I supposed to get to my bedroom without him seeing?" Our cozy three-bedroom house wasn't like the huge mansion that the Sanders' lived in. There was only one way from the bedrooms to the kitchen, and that was to walk through the living room.

"Is there a problem?" DC asked as he walked closer to the kitchen.

Did I mention that our kitchen doesn't have a door? It's right off the dining room, where Detective

Cooper was standing now. I ducked behind the kitchen counter so he wouldn't see me.

"You look fine," Mom said.

For the first time in my entire life, I could tell my mother was lying. But there was no way to get out of this. So I stood up, rinsed my morning coffee breath in the sink, and patted down my hair. I told myself I could handle this with dignity as I headed into the living room wearing my torn pajama bottoms and a baggy t-shirt with no bra. Just the outfit any plus-sized woman would love to greet people in!

———

I WISHED WE WERE SITTING DOWN ON THE couches, but Detective Cooper "preferred to stand." I attempted to angle my body to the right so he wouldn't see the huge tear by the left pocket of my pajama bottoms. But each time I did, the infuriating man shifted his position so he was right in front of me.

"What made you suspect Celia?" I asked.

"I'm the one who asks the questions, ma'am." I wished he'd stop with that ma'am thing.

"Call her Christy," Mom called out from the dining room as she pretended to drink her coffee and read the paper.

"Now, you said earlier that Celia was with you the entire day, with the exception of the time just before you found the body. Is that right?"

"Yes," I said. It took a lot of willpower to answer succinctly, but I noticed that anytime I complicated answers in any way, he would insist on clarifying them. I wanted to get through his questions so I could tell him about the brother.

"If I understand correctly, you and Celia are cousins. Have you known each other your whole lives?"

"I didn't know her personally my whole life, but I knew of her. What I mean is, her family moved to California from the Philippines about twenty years ago. We went to the same high school. So sort of, yes."

"Just to clarify, you've known Celia for roughly twenty years. Is that correct?" he said.

I wanted to slap the man, and he didn't seem to like me that much at this moment either. This interview was going to take forever. I forced myself not to roll my eyes and then I realized he was waiting for an answer. "Yes."

"So that makes you what, 34? 39?" he asked. His voice sounded surprised.

"She's 35, but looks young for her age," Mom called out. "She takes after me." I wanted to throttle her. Thirty-five is not old at all. Then, I noticed for the first time the detective cracked a smile and nodded his head. But then his face turned serious again.

"Has Celia ever spoken about her work to you?" he asked.

Celia bragged about her job all the time and about how much the Sanders Family, especially Mr. Sanders, loved her. Then a horrifying thought struck me. Celia had even bragged about the probability she would wind up in the will.

"Miss Murphy?" he said.

"Christy," Mom corrected.

"I was just trying to remember," I said trying to cover my tracks and then answered, "Yes."

"Yes, what?" he asked, annoyance crept into his tone.

"Yes, she spoke of her job to me."

He shot me a look. When I wanted to give longer answers, he didn't like them, but now he was annoyed that I'd answered simply. "And?" he asked pointedly.

"She talked about how much they liked her. How good she was at the job. She'd even been invited to the birthday party as a guest," I said avoiding the will entirely.

"Did she ever talk about her duties on the job? Like did she administer medication to Harold Sanders?"

I gave a sigh of relief. He didn't know about the will. "I don't know for sure, but I would guess so. She's a registered nurse, and she's been with the family for over five years. She'd take him to the hospital, the pharmacy, and things like that," I said. I didn't know where he was going with this, but he seemed pleased with my answer, which I didn't like.

"Has your cousin mentioned having any knowledge of Harold Sanders' will?" he asked.

Oh no! He knew!

"Shall I take that shocked look as a yes?" he asked.

Shoot! My panic showed. I couldn't lie now, could I? "She'd mentioned it."

"Did she also talk to you about coming into some money soon?" he said, pausing to flip through his notes, "like going on a vacation to Europe?"

Oh no! Celia bragged all over town that she might go to Europe. This wasn't looking good for Celia.

"Does your cousin have a taste for expensive jewelry?" he asked.

"Her jewelry is fake," Mom called out from the dining room.

He nodded at Mom's answer and turned to me for a response.

"I don't know." I said.

"In the twenty some odd years you've known her, would you say she wore jewelry daily?" he asked.

I sighed. "Yes."

"Did she wear the same stuff or different stuff?" he asked.

"Different," I said.

"More than one piece at a time? Like a ring and a necklace?"

"What's all this about?" I asked. "What does this have to do with the murder?"

"It's my job to—"

"I know, I know," I interrupted. "It's your job to ask the questions. Yes she wore different pieces at the same time."

"Have you noticed her wearing a new necklace lately?"

"I've been busy with some personal stuff, so I've only seen her a few times in the last year or so. I don't remember what she was wearing the other times, but on the day of the murder she wore her wedding ring, a gold chain with a cross around her neck, and diamond-stud earrings, but I doubt they were real diamonds."

"And you remember the murder day, because of this memory thing? But you don't remember anything from before that?

"I remember some things, just not as many details." Geez.

"Do you remember seeing her wearing an antique pearl necklace with a jade and diamond clasp?" he asked.

"I didn't see," Mom answered. "And if it were real pearls, I'd notice."

He turned to me. "Me neither."

"That necklace, which belonged to the Sanders' family, was found in your cousin's home last night."

My mind flashed back to the argument Margaret and Mr. Sanders had the day of the murder. Margaret had yelled about her father misplacing an antique pearl necklace. This couldn't be a coincidence.

"I see you remember something," he said.

Geez Louise! He caught my look again. I sighed. Why couldn't he be like those bumbling detectives in the movies? "I remember overhearing Margaret and her father arguing before the party. She said something about him misplacing a necklace." What I didn't want to tell him, and I wouldn't if he didn't ask, was that Mom had specifically asked about the necklace, and Celia had ignored the question. Celia was always a bit sneaky, but I'd never thought she'd steal.

"About this argument," he began as he flipped through his notebook to check his notes. "That would be before the party. Where were you?"

I knew he'd written down on his pad that I was in the kitchen with Celia. Was he checking to see if my story was consistent? "Like I told you before," I said, "I was in the kitchen with Mom and Celia."

He nodded, but for a brief second I saw him smile. He knew that I knew that he was double checking my story. The man had a handsome smile. It almost made me forget how annoyed with him I was.

"Tell me about this argument," he said.

"I'm sure Margaret or Celia must've mentioned it."

"I wouldn't say if they had, but let's talk about what you know."

I realized that anything was better than talking about that necklace. At least this might get him looking into other suspects. So I told him about the fight, and how that gave the daughter motive to kill her dad. Then, Mom piped in and told him about the brother's motive, and how George blamed his father for being sentenced to prison for two years. DC made notes, but he didn't seem as interested in our theories.

"Okay, thanks," he said closing his notebook.

"Can we visit Celia at the station?" I asked.

"No," he said.

"Why the heck not?" I snapped.

He held up his hands in surrender. "Now, don't get upset just yet. She made bail late last night, so I assume she's at home. Okay?"

"Fine," I said as I adjusted my glasses, completely forgetting that I was supposed to be holding closed the gaping hole in my pajamas, until I felt the telltale coolness on a part of my outer thigh I've chosen to keep secret from the world since I was sixteen. I gasped like an idiot and grabbed at my leg.

"What's wrong?" he asked.

I cursed myself for being such a spazz. He went to look at my leg. I turned away, and something rubbed against my ankle. I screamed.

That darn cat shrieked and tried to claw up Detective Cooper's pants to safety.

I jumped away just in time to hear the masculine and competent DC Cooper yelp and jump around, trying to dislodge our new furry friend.

Mom laughed. I tried not to, but couldn't help myself.

Maybe we should keep this cat.

om and I waited at Lucky Dragon
Palace for Celia to meet us. The
restaurant was crowded for the daily
lunch special, so we had to sit in the small office
adjoining the kitchen instead of our usual booth. We
kept the door open for ventilation and to keep the
room from becoming too claustrophobic. My chair
was half in the doorway and half in the kitchen.

I didn't mind being crammed in the back, even
though it was a tight fit. It was more private.
Everyone in town wanted news about the murder.
Fletcher Canyon had always been the kind of place
that knew everybody's business, but information
about Celia's arrest travelled faster than any other

news. People had even called our house trying to get any bit of the juicy details.

"I think it's why the restaurant even more busy today," Wenling said to Mom.

"If I knew murder was so good for business," Mom joked, "I would've asked Celia to kill Christy's husband."

"Wait," Wenling said. "You told me that Christy was a widow."

My brain remembered Celia, and Todd from the newspaper, saying they were sorry about my husband. "Mom, have you been telling people Robert died?"

Mom laughed.

"Mom, that's not funny," I said.

"It's kind of funny," Mom said.

I saw the back door open, and Celia stepped through it wearing giant Jackie O-style sunglasses, a scarf over her head, and her collar popped up. She was so dramatic. She closed the door, took off her glasses, and rushed over to us.

"My dear family! Thank goodness I got here. The press and the people," she said, "they won't leave me alone."

I wanted to roll my eyes, but I didn't. She looked like a Filipina version of Audrey Hepburn in "Charade." I admired how she pulled off "the look." My hair always fell straight. I could put it back in a pony tail or put it back with barrettes. That's it. No messy buns, up dos, braids, perms, ever looked right. And if any hairstylist could pull it off, the look crumbled within days.

"What happened?" Wenling asked, patting the open seat next to her. She didn't hide her excitement to hear the news, but Celia didn't mind.

"They came to my house and arrested me! I was in jail for hours until My Dearest could post bail. It was awful."

"What were you doing with the necklace?" I asked.

"That," Celia waved it off, "is just a simple misunderstanding. Sir Harold wanted me to have it." I could tell she was taking great pains to downplay that it was a big deal.

"But the agency doesn't allow gifts!" Mom said.

"Of course not! I told him. He insisted. So I took it. I figured I would bring it back after the party, return it to the safe, and he would think I had it."

"You have the combination to the safe?" I asked.

Celia smiled. "Sir Harold has me open it for him all the time. He trusts me more than his own daughter."

"Celia, does Mr. Sanders keep a copy of his will in that same safe?" I asked.

She didn't answer.

"Celia," Mom said. "You read that will, didn't you?"

"He wanted me to read it," she said, but her lie wasn't convincing.

"How much did he leave you?" Wenling asked, once again not hiding her excitement.

"He left me the necklace, some money, and a car!" Celia said.

"And your fingerprints are all over that safe," I said.

"Aye!" Mom said knowing what I was getting at.

"How much money?" Wenling asked.

Celia shrugged her shoulders trying to be coy.

"That much," Wenling said, nodding her head. Mom nodded, too.

"I didn't say anything," Celia said.

"I bet it's a half a million," Mom said.

Celia's jaw dropped open. "How did you know?" she asked. That's when my jaw dropped open. How did Mom know?

Mom smiled, but didn't answer Celia's question. I made a note to ask Mom about that later. Although, she still hadn't told me how she convinced Mr. Sanders to agree to the party.

"They think you did it, because of the will, you know," Mom said.

"That and the pills," Celia answered.

"What about the pills?" I asked.

"That's why he was asking about Celia administering medication," Mom said. "Something went wrong with the medication."

"They've already talked to you?" Celia asked, glaring at me.

"DC came by this morning," Mom said.

"The handsome detective came to your house?" Wenling asked not hiding her hurt about not getting the news. "Why didn't you tell me while we were waiting?"

"I didn't want to explain it twice," Mom said.

Wenling was less than impressed with that answer.

Celia interrupted. "What did you say?"

"He talked mostly to Christy," Mom said, totally throwing me under the bus with the truth. Celia turned to me and glared.

"I had to tell the truth, but we told him that we'd never seen you with the necklace,'" I said, leaving out the part where I had to confirm that she'd bragged about going to Europe.

"How could you betray me?" Celia asked, folding her arms.

"I didn't betray you!" I said.

She turned away from me.

"What about the pills?" Mom asked.

"They said that Sir's pills had been half-empty. That someone had opened each of the capsules and poured out the medicine!"

"Why would someone do that?" Wenling asked.

"To kill him," Celia said. "But they think it was me who did it."

"Your fingerprints are probably all over the bottle," I said.

"Of course! I give him his medicine every day. I pick it up from the pharmacy! But why would I pour out the medicine from his pills? I could just substitute different pills, he wouldn't know the difference."

"Someone else had to do it," Mom said. "The son was staying there wasn't he?"

"For three days only," Celia said with disappointment.

"But he could've gotten to the pills," I said.

Celia shook her head. "He might not have died after only three days."

"But maybe," I said.

"Maybe," Celia said sounding dejected.

"Then it's the daughter," I said. "The checkbook was open when I found the body, and they'd fought about it."

"It was there when I went upstairs. That's when Harold paid me," Mom said distracted by her thoughts. "I just don't think," Mom paused. "maybe it was her."

"Her fingerprints might be on the bottle," I added.

"If I were her," Mom said. "I would've poured out the pills, wiped the bottle, and just waited for Celia and Harold to fingerprint it up again."

I nodded. Mom was right.

Jennifer rushed into the kitchen. "Thank God, you're here and you're all right," she said to Celia. "You need to stay away from George?"

"Why?" Celia asked.

"Who's George?" Wenling chimed in.

Mom said, "You know, George. He's Harold's son."

"That George," Wenling said.

Jennifer nodded. "He's really upset about his father's death."

"Or he's just pretending," I said.

Jennifer shook her head no. "You know Barbara's niece, Ann works part-time at The Watering Hole, right?"

"That's no place for her," Wenling said.

Mom nodded her head in agreement. "It's shady."

The Watering Hole was a dive bar in Sylmar, which is the next town over.

Jennifer nodded and then continued her story. "Ann called home to Barbara to tell her if she saw Celia to watch out for George. She came in for the lunch special and told me just now. I didn't tell her you were here, so word doesn't get out."

Celia put her scarf back on, and glasses.

"But why would Celia have to watch out for George?" I asked.

"George was in the bar getting drunk and talking crazy. He said he'd kill Celia if he finds her. He even asked Ann where Celia lives!"

"This is a small town. Everybody knows where everybody lives," I said.

"He can't think I'm the killer!" Celia said. "No one really believes that."

Jennifer looked down. I could tell she must've heard people gossiping who did believe Celia did it. "Maybe you should leave town with your kids."

"The judge said not to leave town," Celia said. "But maybe my kids and husband should go to my mother-in-law's in Arizona."

"That's probably smart," I said.

"Jennifer, tell everyone Celia is off to Arizona with her family, and we'll hide her at our house," Mom said. "Leave your car here so no one will know, and we'll drop you off."

"Where are you guys going?" Celia asked.

"We're going to find out who really killed Harold Sanders," Mom said.

Celia smiled. She seemed to believe we would find the real killer.

I wasn't so confident.

———

FOR A MOMENT I THOUGHT I MIGHT MISS THAT darn cat, but after trying for a half an hour to wrestle him into the van, I was so over it. We headed back up the dreaded mountain to see Margaret, under the pretext of finding the owner for that menace of a tuxedo cat. My catering-van driving skills hadn't improved much, and rush-hour traffic didn't help. Okay, Fletcher Canyon didn't have the traffic problems most of Los Angeles did, but even the few extra cars we had on the road made me nervous. It's one thing to die in a fiery crash off the side of a mountain. It's a whole other thing to take innocent bystanders with you.

"Is that a siren?" I asked Mom as I checked my mirrors and wished, once again, for a rearview window. The noise grew louder.

Mom tilted her head for a listen. "I don't think so."

Panic set in. "There's no place to pull over on this road."

"There's a turnout over here," Mom said and pointed to a very small bit of dirt to the right of the road, next to a death-drop of an edge.

"That wasn't big enough for our van."

"It was the size of two parking spaces."

"It came up too fast."

The siren grew louder, and in my mind, it sounded angrier. I kept trying to see the cop behind us, but all I saw was empty road. He must be right on our tail.

"We're almost at the Sanders' house. Just pull onto their private road and stop," Mom said.

My heart raced. The police already had it in for Celia. Now they'll have it in for me. I pulled onto the private road and shut off the ignition, almost forgetting to engage the emergency brake. Mom and I traded a look. "Sorry," I said.

The siren kept blasting, which annoyed me, because we'd obviously pulled over. I opened the door with my hands up in surrender.

"You don't have to put your hands up," Mom said.

"I don't want them to shoot me for fleeing," I hissed at Mom. Or rather, I didn't hiss, something else did. And that's when I realized it wasn't a siren. It was that darn cat yowling in the back of the van.

Mom suppressed her laugh.

"That cat could've killed us," I said getting back into the van and heading up the road to go to Sanders' house.

"I'm going to miss her when we find her owner," Mom said.

"It's a him," I corrected but Mom didn't answer. She pointed to the open gate. Normally, we'd have to buzz to be let in, this time it was open. I shot Mom a worried look.

"Just drive in," Mom said.

I did what she said, but I didn't like the look of this.

————

THE MOMENT I PARKED THE VAN, THE YOWLING stopped, which took the edge off my worry.

"You get the cat. I'll ring the bell," Mom said.

"That cat hates me," I said.

Mom rolled her eyes. "I'll help you with him."

I paused before opening the back doors of the van, and prepared to use the door as a shield if the cat leapt out and attacked me. Mom rolled her eyes, scooted me out of the way, and opened the doors herself.

The cat yowled. Mom shushed him, and the little thing quieted. "Come on," Mom said to the cat, and the fur ball trotted to the edge of the van and leapt into Mom's arms. "Good cat," Mom said and patted it on the head.

I shook my head and closed the van doors.

We rang the doorbell. Margaret greeted us, but she was obviously expecting someone else.

"I thought you were my psychic," she said.

"Is that why the gate's unlocked?" Mom asked.

"Yes. I didn't want to risk missing her. I desperately need her advice."

"About what?" I asked.

Margaret gave me a shocked look. "The murder of course. I can't believe Celia would have killed my father. And I have to find out who did it before my drunken brother does something stupid."

Mom and I traded glances. "Do you think it's possible your brother did it?" Mom asked.

"I'd thought of that, but he's so upset, and he hasn't been here long enough," Margaret said. Her attention turned to the cat. "What a beautiful cat! Did you bring her in for an evaluation?"

"Yes," Mom said.

Margaret beamed. "Come inside."

"Is this the cat from the party?" Margaret asked.

"Yes," Mom said. "We really like him."

"His coat is very shiny. I'd advise keeping the dear as hydrated as possible so that her fur will look its best when she's preserved."

It took me a moment to realize that we were getting a taxidermy consultation.

"How much longer did the vet give her to live?" Margaret asked.

"It's hard to say. It depends on how well she responds to the medication," Mom answered.

Mom was always a fast thinker. Margaret nodded, but she looked a little disappointed at the idea that the cat might live. Heck, the thing was more of a kitten than a cat. I almost felt bad for the little thing-- almost.

"There's an oil you can use that will keep her fur soft just in case," Margaret said hopefully. I found it interesting that an heiress to a multi-million dollar fortune was so interested in making a sale. "It also is good for preventing flees," she added.

"How much?" Mom asked.

Margaret smiled. "Only twenty dollars," she said.

"We'll take it," Mom said.

Margaret sprang from her seat to get the oil.

"She doesn't seem like a murderer," I said.

"No," Mom said. "If I'd killed my dad to fund a weird animal stuffing business, I wouldn't hire a psychic."

"Me neither," I said.

"Do you have twenty dollars?" Mom asked.

I reached into my purse for my last twenty. "I guess this means we own a cat now."

Margaret returned with the oil and gave us instructions on how to use it.

"Who do you think besides Celia could be a suspect?" Mom asked. I was surprised Mom came right out and asked.

"I have no idea. The only people with access to the pills would be Celia, George, and me. Unless Dad committed suicide, but I doubt that."

Mom nodded. "Me, too."

Even though I knew Mom and Margaret were right, I wished they weren't. Because Celia looked pretty guilty right now.

6

COOKING AND CRIME SOLVING

I'd forgotten it was Monday afternoon until Mom reminded me. On Mondays the restaurant closed early. That's when Mom (and now Mom and I) baked the cakes and almond cookies for the week. I drove down the winding hill while our new cat rested in Mom's lap.

Mom called home to check on Celia. I could tell by what I overheard that Celia was disappointed we hadn't found out more about the real killer. Mom reassured her that we'd figure it out, which worried me.

"How is Celia?" I asked as I turned on Foothill Boulevard.

"She ate leftovers and settled into your room," Mom said.

"My room! What's wrong with the guest room?"

"The window to your room faces the back of the house. She wanted to make sure the press couldn't spy on her," Mom said.

I didn't buy that explanation. The guest room was smaller and doesn't have a TV. I knew Celia chose the better room on purpose, but I let it go. If I were a suspect in a murder, I might need to watch some television to take my mind off of things.

I parked the car behind the restaurant. Mom knocked on the back door. They locked it at sundown.

"Who's there?" Wenling asked.

"Aye!" Mom said. "It's us. What you mean who's there?"

Wenling opened the door. "Jo! Christy! So sorry," she said. "A reporter spotted Celia's car in the back, and he insisted she was here. He kept knocking on this door for like a half hour.

"It's us to bake. It's Monday," Mom said.

That's when Wenling realized she'd been blocking the doorway.

"I forgot," Wenling said, moving out of the way. "You're early."

"We figured we'd have an early dinner and give you the news," Mom said.

Wenling smiled. "Good idea! I'll make coffee. Do you want shrimp? Crab?"

"Wow!" I said. We normally had the special of the day or whatever they had the most of. Since Wenling always refused to let us pay, we never ordered anything extravagant.

Mom mumbled under her breath. "She's buttering us up to get the good gossip."

"I think it's going to work," I said, ready to eat crab.

"Yeah," Mom said and laughed.

———

FLETCHER CANYON WAS A SMALL TOWN WITH

early risers–especially during the week. Mondays were slow, and the few people who came in after lunch ordered take-out. So instead of crowding into the back office, we ate dinner at our usual booth in the back. Wenling even set out a small bowl of milk with a piece of fish for the cat to eat under the table. This made Wenling and the cat instant best friends. Despite having forked over twenty bucks to get that special fur oil for him, the cat only tolerated my presence. We caught up Wenling on what we'd learned visiting Margaret Sanders.

"It looks like Celia might be in serious trouble," Wenling said. "You don't think she did it, did you?"

"She couldn't have," Mom said. "The will isn't that strong a motive to risk prison. He was eighty five years old and on heart medication. All she had to do was wait," Mom said.

"Maybe she has a gambling problem? Or a secret baby stashed somewhere," Wenling said.

"She can't have a secret baby. We would have had to see her pregnant," I said.

"From before she came here then," Wenling said.

"She came to the US when she was fourteen," Mom said.

"That's old enough," Wenling said.

"Then, why would she suddenly need the money now?" I asked.

Wenling considered that idea. "Maybe college? Or the kid is sick?"

"Or maybe there's no secret baby," I said.

"Then, it has to be gambling debts," Wenling said in a solemn tone.

"I don't think so," I said.

"We'd have noticed sooner than this," Mom said. "When you have a gambling problem, you sell your stuff first, not kill your biggest client."

"But she didn't have anything to sell. All her jewelry was fake," Wenling said.

"I know," Mom said shaking her head. "But she had a car."

My mind went to the pearl necklace with the jade

and diamond clasp. I looked up at Mom and she shook her head for me not to say anything.

"Well, it's time to start baking," Mom said, looking at her watch. It was ten minutes to six. We usually started by five, and I was already tired.

Wenling closed the restaurant while we cleared the dishes.

Once she left I said, "You don't think she did it, do you?"

Mom furrowed her brow and mixed the ingredients for the almond cookies in a bowl. "I don't know. We might have to rethink things. I need you to go over everything you remember from the murder."

"Mom, that'll take hours," I said.

"So will this baking. Now get the almond extract while I grab the rolling pin," Mom said.

I dug around the cupboard to find the little bottle. Mom made me get the extract because the chef puts it on the top shelf. He never needs it during the week. I found it shoved behind some soy sauce that had to have been there for thirty years, it was so thick. I walked over to the bowl to add it.

You know how you sometimes smell something, and it reminds you of when you were a kid? For me candy apples always reminded me of Halloween in elementary school. Well, the second I got a whiff of the almond extract my mind flashed back to the murder scene.

"What's wrong?" Mom asked.

I guess I must've had a funny look on my face.

"I just remembered finding Mr. Sanders. The room smelled a little like this stuff," I said holding up the bottle.

Mom's eyes grew wide.

"What?" I asked.

She didn't answer and whipped out her cell phone.

"Who are you calling?" I asked.

"DC," Mom said.

———

"THIS BETTER BE GOOD," THE DETECTIVE SAID when Mom let him in through the back door of the restaurant. I busied myself pressing almonds into the tops of the latest batch of cookies before they cooled.

"Don't put the next batch into the oven," Mom said to me. "He's here."

I finished up with the cookies just as Mom brought DC over.

"Okay, tell him now," Mom said.

I shot Mom a panicked look. She's the one who called him over, and now I was the one who had to talk to him.

"About the smell," Mom said.

"Oh," I said. "There was a faint smell of almonds in the room."

"I didn't smell anything like that when I got in there," he said.

I closed my eyes and replayed the moment in my mind. "It was when I tried to give him CPR after I called 911 from the telephone. His breath. It smelled a little like almond extract, but very light."

Mom gave the detective a look that said, "See, I told you this was important."

"That only happens in movies," he said to Mom, but I didn't know what they were talking about.

"What?" I asked. "What's the big deal about the smell."

"It means anybody at the party could have killed Mr. Sanders," Mom said.

"How?" I asked.

"Cyanide poisoning," Mom said.

"How do you know it was cyanide poisoning?" I asked.

"Every crime show watcher and mystery reader knows that cyanide gives off a faint smell of bitter almonds," Mom answered.

"It still could've been Celia," the detective said. "And why would she empty out half of the pills just to put cyanide in some of them? There couldn't have been enough cyanide in the pills to have the onset occur so suddenly."

"But anyone could have poisoned the drink he used to wash down the pills," Mom said.

The detective whipped out his notebook and rifled

through his notebook. "Let's see what he had to drink," he said.

But I didn't have to wait for him to look it up.

"He had a diet soda," I said.

"And where did he get that?" Detective Cooper asked.

I didn't have to search my memory for that answer either. "I gave it to him."

7

BREAKING BREAD

The next morning, I woke up in our guest room (my younger and more successful brother's former room) disoriented and stressed. After one day of investigating, Mom and I had detective-worked ourselves into the role of suspects. Of course, I was more of a suspect than Mom. And Celia wasn't off the hook either. Celia, ever the kind cousin, had been good enough to take all of my things from what used to be my bedroom, and put them in the closet for me. It made me wonder how long she planned on staying.

Some of Dad's old clothes were here. I spotted what looked like the leather jacket my brother, sister, and I chipped in to get him for Christmas (with Mom's considerable help). It was seventy-five degrees in

California the Monday after the holiday break, but Dad still wore that leather jacket to work. I stepped further back into the closet to look at it, and I noticed grandpapa's old briefcase on the floor behind some shoes. I hadn't seen it since Aunt Lalaine brought it back from the Philippines when I was in high school. How did it get here?

The case was slightly open, and I reached down to close it. Some of the papers got in the way of the latch. I opened it to push them aside. That's when I spotted what looked like a police report from Lapi-tan, a small municipality in the province of Negros Oriental where my mother grew up. It was written in English, like most government documents in the Philippines are, and it detailed Aunt Lalaine's auto accident. Except, there weren't many details at all. It said that she died in an auto accident and the date, but not much else.

I looked through the briefcase. There were photos and notes. Who had gathered all of this? Mom hadn't been to the Philippines in over a decade. Not since-- oh wait--she'd gone back for Aunt Lalaine's funeral. Had Mom been investigating her death?

"Oh no!" Celia shouted from the living room.

I shoved the papers back into the case, closed it, and rushed into the living room.

I expected to see her covered in blood or at the very least holding a stubbed toe, but instead she was just standing by the front door holding the newspaper.

"Don't put that newspaper anywhere near the sofa," Mom warned.

Growing up, our family living room had been a study in brown, our dark wood floor matched beige curtains and a boring brown sofa. But Mom's redecorating had added a white, linen sofa with clean lines, an elegant glass coffee table, and elegant long white curtains with silver trim. I imagine she never would have dared have so much white with three kids and a husband who liked to eat Cheetos while he watched football.

"That man from the Valley News who I dodged yesterday wrote a story about me, and look at the photo!"

Celia turned the paper around to show us the large photo. It was taken when Celia was in her Audrey Hepburn getup, but the photographer had snapped the picture when Celia's head was looking down and her mouth was open. It made her look like she had a double chin and a slack jaw. Even I felt bad for her. Then I read the story, and it was even worse.

Celia's cell phone rang. Her face turned even more sad. "I'm innocent until proven guilty," Celia said to the person on the telephone. She listened for a minute and then said, "I appreciate your call and support," but I could tell from her tone and frown that she didn't mean it. She hung up.

"Who was that?" Mom asked.

"Jess from church. They won't be needing anything from me for the charity auction. She said she didn't want to burden me at this difficult time."

Mom shook her head no.

"Sorry Celia," I said and put my hand on her shoulder. She smiled back at me.

The three of us headed for the kitchen for coffee. Mom filled Celia in on what we discovered talking to Margaret, and told her about the cyanide theory. Celia seemed glum until Mom told her about our talk with DC.

"So we're all potential murderers?" Celia asked with a smile.

"Yes, especially you and Christy," Mom answered, glad to see that something had cheered up my cousin. I guess misery does enjoy company. I grabbed a diet soda from the refrigerator to go with my half-caff coffee. It was setting up to be that kind of day.

"When do you guys get arrested?" Celia asked.

"They have to do an autopsy and find out if there really was cyanide poisoning," Mom said, not at all concerned about our impending doom.

"You knew it was murder all along!" Celia said. "Maybe you're psychic."

"I'm not psychic," Mom said with a smile. "There's no such thing."

I didn't believe in psychics either, but it would explain how Mom was always right. Although, perhaps that's just the nature of motherhood. I think there's a saying about moms and being right.

"Tell me about Harold's girlfriend. Where does she live? We need to see her today," Mom said.

"What makes you think Mr. Sanders had a girl-friend?" I asked Mom, sitting down at the kitchen table. Celia ignored me and answered Mom.

"You think Edna killed him? But why? He wanted to marry her," Celia said.

Celia's talk about marriage triggered my memory.

"Everyone's a suspect, but if anyone knows Harold's secrets, it Edna. Has she known him a long time?" Mom asked.

"Wait!" I said as my mind played back some of the things on Harold's desk. "Is that why he had cruise brochures on his desk?"

Celia's eyes brightened up. "For their honeymoon. Ma'am Edna mentioned taking an Alaskan cruise once, so he thought it would be nice to take her. The great thing Mr. Sanders said about Ma'am Edna is she's already rich, so he knew she wouldn't be trying to marry him for his money."

"I knew it," Mom said.

"What?" I asked.

"When I went up to talk to him about having the

party, I mentioned that there had to be a special guest he didn't want to disappoint. That's what changed his mind."

"He was going to ask Edna to marry him this week," Celia said.

"How do you know that?" I asked.

"He's been following her around town for the last year since her husband died," Celia said. "He's trying to woo her. I think it's working."

"I think it's stalking," I said.

"Does Edna mind?" Mom asked. She seemed a little wary, too.

"We run our errands on the days she does, hoping to run into her. And they talk. Sometimes he takes her out for coffee. She doesn't seem to mind."

"Are you always there?" I asked.

"I make an excuse sometimes so they can be alone. And last week, Sir and I devised a plan to figure out her ring size. When I saw her last week, I asked her to try on my ring on her left hand, because I thought we had the same size fingers. And we did! I told her I forgot my ring's size, and I wanted to order a ring online, but I needed to know my size. She said hers was a six. So Sir bought a beautiful ring. It arrived the day before the party."

"But she's still wearing her old wedding ring," I said. "Or at least she was at the party."

Mom looked down at her ring finger. Dad died almost six years ago, but it took a while for Mom to stop wearing her ring. "I don't think Edna was ready to remarry." Mom's face looked so sad. I needed to distract her.

"I take it we're going to Edna's house," I said to Mom. She nodded yes. "I'll go and get dressed then." As I left the kitchen, I heard Mom ask Celia what medication Harold Sanders was on. My brain flashed an image of the pill bottle on the floor and called out, "Altonquin." I went back to the guest room to get dressed and spotted the briefcase again. I'd have to ask Mom about that later.

———

FLETCHER CANYON WAS A SMALL ENOUGH TOWN

that Mom and I knew that Edna lived on Daniel Street, but weren't sure which house it was.

"It's either that one or the other big one we passed a few minutes ago," Mom said. "Just park here, and we'll knock on both." Mom pointed to a space on the curb, but all my brain could think was "Mayday! Mayday! Parallel parking attempt! Prepare for disaster."

Seventeen excruciating turns of the wheel later, the van was parked somewhere in the vicinity of the curb, and no other cars were harmed in the process. Victory!

"Good job!" Mom said, and I don't even think she was being sarcastic.

Mom and I approached the bigger house. Mom checked the mailbox: Edna Fisher. Aha!

I found myself nervous about the idea of walking up to the house unannounced. I hesitated for a moment, but Mom did not. She marched straight up the brick path that led to the front door. I had no choice but to follow.

The older, ranch style home was well kept. It sat on

at least two acres of property and was set far back from the road. The yard wasn't fenced in, but it did have a lovely high hedge along the perimeter, and the distance from the street allowed for privacy. My guess was it was like the Sanders Family, The Fishers sold off portions of their former farmland, and the rest of the houses in the neighborhood were built around it.

Mom rang the doorbell, and Edna answered the door.

"Hi, Edna," Mom said.

"Jo!" Edna said. "What a wonderful surprise."

My entire body relaxed as the two talked.

"I'm sorry I didn't call to get together for lunch, but I thought with your niece--" Edna paused.

"It's all right," Mom said. "Actually, my daughter and I might be suspects in the murder now. We need to ask you questions so we don't go to jail."

Mom's bluntness amazed me. I think it might have taken Edna by surprise as well, but it worked. Edna invited us in, and within minutes were in her dining room drinking coffee and having fresh-baked bread.

———

Edna poured another round of coffee as the talk of bread baking subsided.

"I know the circumstances of your visit are glum, but I do appreciate the company," Edna said.

"Christy just moved back in to help me with the catering business—"

"And Mom is helping me out while I go through my divorce," I interrupted. I appreciated Mom trying to make me look good, but the truth was Mom was helping me out, not the other way around.

"But before that," Mom continued, "the house was so quiet. I'd leave the television on to hear the noise."

Edna laughed. "I just had it on when you rang the bell!"

"Harold Sanders wanted to keep you company," Mom said.

Edna sighed.

"He wanted too much too soon, didn't he?" Mom asked.

"I don't know about that," Edna said. "I suspected he might want something more, but I couldn't be sure."

"He was going to propose to you," I said.

Edna's eyes widened. "I don't believe that. That's just a rumor."

"What makes you say that?" Mom asked.

"We only saw each other around town. We'd get coffee while Celia ran errands. But it wasn't anything serious." Edna shook her head. "This town is full of so much gossip. If they see two people eating together, they think they've got to be a couple."

Mom nodded at me to go ahead and tell Edna. "Celia told us that she helped Harold buy the ring. I even saw cruise brochures on his desk. I think he was planning a honeymoon."

Edna shook her head. "That old fool. I'd mentioned thinking about taking an Alaskan cruise, but he couldn't have bought a ring. That can't be right."

"Celia said she got your ring size by having you try on her wedding ring last time they ran into you," Mom said.

"Oh my," Edna said looking down at her own ring. "That's what that was about." Edna exhaled. Her mouth in a frown. "What's with men these days, anyway?"

"I'm in the middle of a divorce," I said. "Exasperation with men is a topic I can talk about for years."

Edna smiled.

"I take it Harold wasn't the only man giving you a hard time," Mom said.

"It'll sound like I'm bragging, but it's probably just about my money."

"Harold was pretty rich on his own," I said.

"Harold was just lonely. It was Charles that needed the money. Years ago the three of us would hang out after school, but only in private."

"Why?" Mom asked.

"I'm Jewish. Nobody thought much about it when we first moved to town. There weren't any synagogues here back then, but when we had a death in the family word spread. Back in those days, things were different. Most of the kids in high school avoided me for the rest of the year. Harold and Charles would talk to me in secret. At first I was just glad for the company, but then I just got tired of it. My parents saw what a hard time I was having and sent me to boarding school. I only moved back here a year ago after my husband died," she sniffed.

"The first few years after my husband died I'd wake up and think he was still alive," Mom said.

"I've had that same thing," Edna said.

Mom and I had talked about Dad a lot over the last five years, but I'd never seen her like this--relating widow to widow.

Mom took Edna's hand. "It hurts less over time, but don't listen to anyone who says 'it's time to move on.' You take as much time as you need. Forever if you want."

Edna smiled. "Thanks."

They traded tidbits about life alone and TV shows, and I listened.

Listening to them, I realized that for so much of my life I looked at my mom as my mom, the person who raised me. The one who embarrassed me in middle school by making me carry an old Smurf lunchbox on a school field trip. The woman who solved my problems and fixed my hair. I was a kid, and she was the grown-up in charge.

And then I got absorbed in my own life and troubles, and even though I'd become a grown woman, I still saw her as Mom. But seeing her comforting Edna, it struck me how incredible my mother was, not just as my mom, but as a woman.

If I'd met her at a party or around town, I would want to talk to her just like everyone else does. No wonder she makes friend with people wherever she goes, and people always tell her their secrets and seek her advice. She empathized with people and listened with her whole heart. And Mom was fun.

"So Charles came around, too," Mom said.

"He came by today to give me these photos he framed of the flowers in my garden," Edna said as she reached over and grabbed the stack. I'd baked the bread and made coffee for him actually."

Edna handed one photo to me and one to Mom. The other rested on the table. Mom's was a closeup of a butterfly on a flower, and mine was a pink rose bush. Mom's looked more interesting.

"I like this," Mom said.

"I think it's the best of the three. Between you and me, he just got lucky with the butterfly. I watched him take it. The thing just flew into the picture, and he snapped it. The rose photo is a bit cliche. The composition isn't very interesting, and the focus is off," Edna said.

"He didn't stay for the bread?" Mom asked.

"No, we got into a bit of a tiff."

"You didn't tell him the truth about his mediocre photography did you?" Mom asked.

Edna laughed. "Oh no! Although he was such a jerk I almost wish I had."

Mom and I laughed. Edna was such a proper lady, it was funny to hear her criticize something and call a guy a jerk.

"What did he want?" Mom asked when our laughter subsided.

"He wanted to talk about moving back to town to

keep me company," she said. "He even had the nerve to ask if he could stay here with me. But I knew what he was up to."

"What?" Mom asked.

"He'd called me when my husband died and sent flowers, but he was a little too flirty on the telephone. When I heard he was coming to town I googled him," Edna said.

"Googles is so great! That and Siri. They know every-thing," Mom said.

I smiled. I always thought to was funny how Mom added an "s" to Google.

"I found out that Charles had gone through a bitter divorce. His former wife inherited an orange grove from her father, and he was running it and stealing from her. She got him kicked out of his job, and with their prenup he got zilch. He was broke and looking for a meal ticket."

"How did you turn him down?" Mom asked.

"I told him I wasn't up to dating anyone, but he didn't believe me."

"Why not?" I asked.

"He'd heard the same rumors you two did about me dating Harold. I told him the same thing I told you, but he insisted that Harold had planned to marry me. I said it was ridiculous, but now I guess he was right. No wonder he was so mad and stormed out of here saying he was going back to Florida."

Mom's eyes widened. "Did he develop and print these pictures himself?"

"He made a big production out of telling me how he'd set up his old darkroom just to print them for me. I didn't want to say anything, but I was an art major in school and his photos aren't worth all that trouble. He'd be better off with a digital camera and printing them out on an inkjet printer. Save his lungs from all those chemicals. He's using all the leftover equipment his daughter keeps for him in the attic. That stuff has got to be from the seventies."

"Do you know where he's staying?" Mom asked.

"He's at Angela Hardy's house. That's his grand-daughter's married name. I doubt he'd be leaving town right away though. He's supposed to speak at

Harold's funeral. Although, now with the delay because of the autopsy, he might not stay."

"How do you know about the autopsy?" Mom asked.

"Margaret called me this morning to say the funeral would be delayed, because the coroner's office needed to run more tests on the body."

"Charles was here when you got the call?" Mom asked.

"Yes, I told him," Edna said.

"I hate to rush off, but we've got to go," Mom said.

Edna stood up and showed us out. "Next time we speak, you'll have to tell me all about working on that show. It sounds so exciting."

When Mom didn't take the opening to talk about her big scene when she was pregnant with me, I knew we were in a rush. Mom was worried that Charles would leave town, which meant Mom thought he was our killer.

Mom talked to Detective Cooper as I sped to Angela Hardy's house. Of course it had to be located up Marple Drive when we were in a hurry. I tried to remain calm, but between the Southern California sun beating through the windshield and the pressure of trying to catch a murderer who might be on the run, stress sweat flowed in an unflattering manor down my face and back.

"Meet us there," I heard Mom say as she hung up.

"What did the detective say?" I asked Mom.

"He said he'd check it out, and we shouldn't go over there."

"Maybe he's right. It's not like we can stop Charles from leaving, and if he's the murderer it can't be a good idea to ask him for all the murderous details ."

"We'll just check if he's there, and if he tries to leave, we'll follow him so DC knows where he is," Mom said.

"Detective Cooper is coming, right?" I asked.

"I think he was going to check it out later, but now that I said we're going over there, I think he might hurry."

"That's not reassuring," I said.

"You're getting better at driving," Mom said changing the subject.

"What makes you say that?" I asked as I turned onto Marple Drive. I'm a sucker for a compliment.

"This is the longest conversation we've had in the van since we got it," Mom said.

I would have laughed, but my driving hadn't improved to the point where I could laugh and steer up a mountain road at the same time.

We turned off of Marple onto the unmarked dirt road with Angela Hardy's house and the homes of her two cousins.

I pulled up onto the shoulder under a tree and parked. "How do we know if he's here?" I asked Mom.

"I don't know," Mom said. "The driveway is empty, but the cars could be in the garage."

"Maybe he's already gone," I said.

"I'll go knock on the door," Mom said.

I grabbed her by the shoulder. "Oh no you don't, Nancy Drew. You're staying right here. If he's the killer, that's dangerous. And if he's not, it doesn't matter."

Mom didn't look happy.

"Mom, we'll stakeout the house and follow him like you said. And if he's gone, then he's gone."

"But if he's gone, we'll need to tell DC to meet him at the airport," Mom said.

"How do we know which airport? And what if he just rented a car to drive home or took the bus? I mean he's broke, right?"

Mom thought about it. "I guess a stakeout is best. But," Mom stopped herself from finishing her thought.

"Go ahead," I said.

"I don't think you'll do well in a car chase."

She had me there.

"What makes you so sure Charles is the murderer?" I asked changing the subject.

"There's a form of cyanide that they used to use in developing pictures, for one," Mom said. "And then there's the part where he'd heard about Harold and Edna dating and getting married. He couldn't have learned that from gossip."

"Why not?"

"He's only been in town for four days, and Celia told us it was a secret."

"Yes, but you know this town and secrets."

"Exactly! I know this town and all the secrets," Mom said.

It took me a moment to figure out what she meant. "Of course! You didn't know about Harold wanting to propose, and we're related to Celia. There's no way a man who's been out of town for over fifty years could get the scoop on gossip that big before you!"

Mom nodded. "And remember Charles saying to DC that he stopped by to see Harold the day before the party and how healthy Harold seemed."

"That was the same day they got the ring!" I said.

"Harold must've been so excited about the ring that he told his old friend about the engagement," Mom said.

I was going to say something, but I noticed Mom looking in her side mirror.

"There's a car coming," Mom said.

I looked out my window, but didn't see anything. "Where?"

"Roll down the window and look at that house over there," Mom said, her voice filled with urgency.

I turned the key so I could use the electric windows, but Mom couldn't wait that long. She jumped out of the van and ran over to take a look.

By the time I got my window open she'd already saw what she'd wanted to.

"It's an Uber!" Mom said. "Quick block the way!"

"How do you know it's an Uber?" I asked.

"Hurry," Mom said. "He'll realize he's at the wrong house, and then he'll go over to Angela's!"

I tried to question Mom, but she pleaded with me to, "Make a U-turn, turn around."

I put the van in drive and pulled forward. Mom cleared out of the way as I turned the wheel hard to the left. The dirt road was so small that I couldn't make it all the way around. The unevenness of the darn road didn't help either. Panicked from trying to hurry, I maneuvered the stick shift into what I hoped was reverse and promptly stalled out.

Mom dashed up to the window of the van. "Good job, kid! Pretend like you can't start it," she said and tossed her cellphone into my lap. "Call DC, tell him to hurry while I stall."

My acting skills are shoddy at best, but pretending to be an incompetent, flustered catering van driver wouldn't be much of a stretch.

The car Mom spotted drove up to my van. Mom ran up to him.

"Mrs. Murphy!" the guy yelled out the window as Mom approached his car. I shouldn't have been surprised. Mom knew everyone in Fletcher Canyon.

Then it occurred to me, if Mom was right about the Uber, then Charles was still at the house and trying to leave. I grabbed Mom's phone, looked up DC's number, and hit call just as I spotted Charles putting his suitcases in the driveway. Could he see his Uber on the other side of my van?

DC picked up. "Please be close by," I said.

"Do not engage with the suspect. This is a matter for the police," he said.

"Mom is out of the van talking to Charles's Uber driver. I don't know what she's doing, but your suspect is trying to flee the area."

"Then I suggest you and your mother get to safety," he said.

The man was so infuriating. "Will you answer one question one darn time? Are you on your way or not?" I said, my voice shrill with panic.

"I'm fifteen minutes away. I need you and your mother to be safe, okay?"

The concern in his voice took me off guard, but then Charles approached the van. I tossed the phone into the passenger seat.

"I need you to move this van," the man said, "I'm expecting—"

That's when I noticed the Uber driver driving away. Charles darted around the van to run after the Uber.

"I stalled out. Give me a minute," I yelled after him, hoping to distract him. He turned back to me and his Uber turned the corner.

Mom came back to the van. Charles stopped her.

"Excuse me, I saw you talking to that driver. Do you know if that car was looking for 4 Mountainside Road?" he asked. "The street isn't marked."

"Yes," Mom answered.

"Well, this is 4 Mountainside," he said. "I guess I'll just call him back."

Rats! The driver couldn't be more than a minute away.

Mom stopped Charles. "He got called away and said to tell you he's sorry."

"I guess the app will just send another car," Charles said squinting to see his cell phone. "I must've left my glasses in the house."

"I'll do it for you," Mom said.

"No, that's all right. I'll call from the house," he said .

"No," Mom stalled. "We'll give you a ride. Pull the van up to the house, kid."

"Wait a minute, aren't you from the party?" Charles said. My stomach turned under they tension.

"Yes!" Mom said. "It'll take ages for another Uber to get here. Fletcher Canyon isn't exactly on the way to many places. Solomon is the only driver who lives in town, and he drives for all of those car places."

The man shook his head. "I don't want to miss my plane. Would a cab get here within the hour?"

"No," Mom said simply. "I'm surprised you're not staying for the funeral," Mom said as she and Charles walked back toward the house. I could kill her. She was going to interrogate the man!

But they were already walking to the house. I had no choice but to start up the van and follow them. It took a billion small turns to get the van going in the right direction and into the driveway, but I did it. Charles had gone inside.

I rushed out of the van and over to Mom. "What are you doing?"

"Is DC on the way?"

"He said he was about fifteen minutes away," I said.

"Then we'll just stall," Mom said.

"Doing what?" I asked.

Mom's eyes widened with delight. "We can crash the van."

"Are you crazy? We're on the side of a mountain, we could die. Heck, he could throw us off that drop right over there," I said as I pointed to the steep drop about forty yards away from the van just to the right of Angela Hardy's house.

"He's not strong enough to drag both of us," Mom said.

"Me, maybe not, but you're not even a hundred pounds," I said. "But he is old. Maybe I could take him in a fight."

"What brings you ladies out here, anyway?" Charles asked as he exited the house with another suitcase. He startled me, but I don't think he heard our whispering.

"I heard you might be moving back to town," Mom said.

Mom thought faster on her feet than anyone. I was busy trying to size up whether I could wrestle Mom away from this guy if he went all murder-y on us.

"Where did you hear that?" Charles asked. His tone was cautious.

"You told me at the party!" Mom said with a laugh.

Charles laughed back. "I'd forgotten." Then he

thought about it and said, "but I still don't understand why you're here."

"I thought that since you hadn't lived here in a while and you weren't married, you might appreciate going out to lunch. But it looks like you're heading out of town. I figured at least we could give you a ride, and perhaps we can have lunch when you get back."

I watched as Charles blushed under Mom's attention. "Well that's nice of you, but it looks like I'm going to stay in Florida."

"That's a shame," Mom said.

"Yeah, it is," Charles said, and he genuinely sounded sad. "Are you sure you're okay with giving me a ride? LAX is pretty far."

"It's no problem," Mom answered. "You can put your luggage in the back." She took the keys from me and walked over to the van to unlock the back door.

"Is your daughter going to come out to say goodbye?" I asked.

"No, she's at work," he said throwing the luggage into the van. The suitcases looked heavy, and he didn't seem to have a problem lifting them. My self esteem sank as I realized that I had a high chance of losing in a physical altercation with someone five decades my senior.

I spotted an old white Ford pickup park on the street, and DC stepped out of it. He'd come on his day off. I felt guilty and relieved. I nudged Mom, and she gave me a quick nod letting me know she'd seen DC as well.

"You seem so nice," Mom said to Charles as she shut the van doors and turned the key to lock it. "It's a shame you poisoned Harold Sanders like that."

My mouth dropped open as did Charles's. Mom walked back toward the driver's side of the van. He followed, his attention focused on Mom. He didn't notice DC coming up the drive.

"I don't know what you're talking about," he stammered.

"Did you leave the poison in the darkroom or is it in your suitcase?" Mom asked.

The look on his face told us the answer. "Give me that key," Charles said, stepping closer to Mom. DC stood right next to me just a few feet from Mom, but

Charles's back was to DC now. Smart move on Mom's part stepping to the side of the van, but I didn't like this dangerous line of questioning.

"I saw you go upstairs before Edna arrived at the party," Mom said. "You said you were lost, but Celia said you were over the day before. The day he got the ring for Edna."

"I should have known she'd never marry that grouchy old fool. He was so sure of himself."

"And you killed him," Mom said.

"You can't prove a thing," Charles said.

"But I think I can," DC interrupted.

Charles's jumped at the sound of DC's voice.

"You should confess," Mom said putting her arm on Charles' shoulder. "The guilt must be unbearable."

The man burst into tears like a little boy. "I'd loved Edna forever. He'd always had his family's money. It made life so easy for him. When I heard she was single, I thought after all these years I had a shot. But he stole it!" Charles sobbed.

"So you went to the party," Mom said.

I shot an incredulous look at DC, and he widened his eyes in amazement. My mother was coaxing this killer into confessing, just like she did with me when I ate cookies before dinner as a kid.

"I put it in his drink. The second he swallowed it I regretted it. He thought he was having some kind of heart attack. He reached for his pills. I fled downstairs. A part of me hoped that someone would find him and call the ambulance in time."

The man dissolved into tears. DC placed him under arrest and put him in the truck before coming over to say goodbye to us. "I told you not to engage with the suspect, you know." His voice wasn't too stern.

"It wasn't me. It was Mom," I said.

"We just offered him a ride to the airport," Mom said.

Detective Cooper shook his head. Mom handed me the keys to the van and said, "Unlock the door so DC can get the suitcases."

"Oh right," I said. I'd forgotten all about the luggage. I walked over to the back of the van, and DC followed me, but Mom didn't. DC stood next to me as I opened the doors and moved out of the way. He leaned into the van and grabbed the suitcases. He was so close I could smell the faint musky scent of his aftershave combined with the clean scent of soap.

I closed the van as he effortlessly pulled out the suitcases and walked them over to his truck. Was I the only person who struggled with heavy luggage?

I took a moment to admire DC's biceps while he put the luggage into the back of his truck. He turned and waved goodbye.

"Come by and see us at the restaurant sometime," Mom said.

DC looked right at me and said. "I'll have to do that."

My face heated, and I fought like mad not to smile like a goofy teenager, but his look turned my limbs to mush.

We watched him drive away and stood there for a minute. Mom broke the silence. "Let's get home and tell Celia she's not going to jail," Mom said.

"Good idea," I said, and we headed for the van. Even though the case was settled and the murderer confessed, I felt like there was a detail we were missing. But then we were driving down the mountain, and I forgot what it was I couldn't remember.

As I PULLED INTO THE DRIVEWAY, I REMEMBERED something. "Mom, did you say the Uber driver's name was Solomon?"

Mom nodded and took off her seatbelt and opened the door.

"You mean the same Solomon who gave you a ride all the way to Hollywood to come visit me?"

"Yes, he goes to Mission Hills College. He's nice," she said and hopped out of the car.

I followed her to our front door. "Mom, you told me your friend Solomon was going to Hollywood, and that's why you were coming for lunch."

"He was," Mom smiled.

"He was because you used the app and had him drive you there. That was expensive, Mom," I said. Mom was on a fixed income because she opted to wait another eight years until she was 65 to collect her small pension from SAG and Dad's teamster pension. The house was paid for, and she had savings, but she needed the money from the catering and the occasional acting/extra job (yes, she still got those every once in a while) for expenses.

"You needed to get out of there," Mom said as we entered the house.

Celia walked into the living room from the hallway. She must've been in my room watching television. Thank goodness she'd be able to go home soon. I wanted my room back.

My room. So weird. I felt at home again, but was that a good thing? Was it a good idea for a woman my age to get comfortable sponging off her mother?

Mom began to tell Celia all about Charles and how he was the killer. Celia was so relieved.

"It's a shame everybody doesn't know I'm not the killer," Celia said. "I know people have been talking. Even people at my church!"

"Don't worry. We'll take care of it," Mom said. "We'll get dressed up, go down to Main Street with our heads held high, and spread the true gossip like there's no tomorrow."

"Do you think that will work?" Celia asked.

"We'll have dinner at Wenling's and then go next door for ice cream. We'll have home court advantage."

Celia looked a little scared. She'd been suspended from her job pending the investigation, and I'm sure she missed her kids. We'd had our differences, but she didn't deserve to be shunned. "Mom's right," I said. "We'll show everyone. You'll be the most popular person in town. Maybe even the newspaper will come down and get your story."

Celia got excited. "I'll change into something nice. Everybody will be looking," Celia said and dashed down the hallway.

"I think I'll change, too," I told Mom.

"I'll feed the cat," Mom said. I'd almost forgotten we had a cat.

"Ice cream is on me! I'm going to inherit a half a million dollars, soon!" Celia called out from my room.

I didn't have the heart to tell Celia that it would take awhile before she got her inheritance, and besides, why give up on free ice cream? I opted to wear my baggier jeans so I could order a double scoop after dinner and hoped Mom was right about convincing the town that Celia was innocent.

———

Mom told me to park on Main Street at one of the open meters instead of parking in the back. "We want everyone to see we're not sneaking around."

"Right," I said feigning confidence I didn't have. I worried this plan might backfire, and, of course, I wasn't a fan of parallel parking. There was a spot on the end of the street, and after nicking the curb a mere three times, I parked the van. If Mom wanted to make sure everyone saw us, the loud noise of the van's hubcaps scraping against the curb and me grinding the gears aided our cause considerably.

I glanced over to Mom seated on the hump of the van, and then to Celia by the window. "Ready guys?"

Celia flipped down the vanity mirror, checked her hair, and said, "Let's do this."

Mom and I nodded, and we all got out of the van. As we made our way up Main Street, Mom spotted Todd Fletcher from the paper.

"Todd! Thanks for coming!" Mom called out. "Have we got a scoop for you!"

Celia held her chin high, and I smiled. Mom must've texted Todd while we were getting dressed. I could almost hear the collective head snap of everyone on the street.

Mom being confident enough to shout out to the editor-in-chief of our town paper made everyone take notice. Todd was a well-respected man in the community. He'd been a top reporter for a national wire service before choosing to retire back here in Fletcher Canyon. His great, great grandfather founded the town back in 1892.

Todd followed us inside Lucky Dragon, and I could feel Celia's reputation rebuilding with each step.

Instead of our table in the back, Mom asked Jennifer if we could eat at the table in the front widow. Celia sat down first in the seat closest to the window. A few minutes later, Jess entered the restaurant with a few other women. Celia smiled and waved. They waved back, but then whispered amongst each other. Celia stayed strong.

Wenling joined us after putting our order in, and Mom, Celia and I told Todd everything. Some of the big daily newspapers in Los Angeles tried to get Todd to work for them, but he always turned them down. Despite our little town paper only coming out once a week, Todd covered his beat so well, he scooped the dailies from time to time, and he was going to do it again with this story.

"This is great," Todd said after all his questions were answered. "I put the paper to bed an hour ago, but it looks like I'll go back in and wake it up. Now, I just need to get confirmation from someone at the police station."

"Detective Cooper is meeting us here to celebrate," Mom said.

"He is?" I asked.

"I texted him when you guys were getting ready. He just texted me back, he'll be here soon," Mom said.

"Great," Todd said and ordered a green tea with no sugar.

I wished I'd put on some makeup and regretted wearing my fat pants.

"Here he is!" Mom said as the detective came inside. The entire restaurant turned to look.

Detective DC Coooper was wearing a light gray shirt that brought out his blue eyes and hugged his shoulders in all the right places. I wondered if he'd worn it for me.

"Come here and celebrate with us!" Mom said.

His face went from smiling to serious. "There may not be cause to celebrate," he said.

Mom's plan had worked perfectly. The restaurant had packed with people who wanted to get the gossip. Although, now the plan looked like it would backfire on us.

"Nonsense," Mom said. "You have the killer. He confessed. He wanted to marry Edna, but thought Harold Sanders would marry her. Even though she wasn't interested in either of them."

"Yes, but there is still a detail we need to clarify regarding your niece," the detective said looking around. "Maybe we can do this somewhere more private."

Celia's face reddened, but she kept a smile plastered on her face. I caught Jess's smirk in my peripheral vision.

"Nonsense," Mom said. "Ask away!"

"It's a matter of the medication," DC said. "I'm afraid Celia is still on the hook for tampering with Harold Sanders' medication."

Oh no! That's the detail I'd forgotten.

The restaurant was silent except for the whispering at Jess's table. People didn't bother to hide their eavesdropping. Everyone's eyes fixed on us.

Mom shook her head. "She didn't tamper with Harold's medication," Mom said.

"I didn't!" Celia said. "He'd try to skip it, but I'd never let him."

"But the fact remains that all the pills in his prescription bottle had half, if not almost all, the medicine poured out of them, and then recapped," DC said. "And your niece and Harold's fingerprints are the only ones on the bottle. They've both handled it so many times even the pharmacy employee's prints were smudged off."

"There's a perfectly logical explanation about his medication," Mom said, allowing her voice to carry throughout the restaurant.

DC smiled. His dimples made him look even cuter when he smiled. I'd never noticed them before. "I'll bite, Jo. Who tampered with Harold's medication?"

"Harold Sanders did it himself," Mom said.

"Harold?" DC asked. "Do you have proof he was suicidal or something?"

"No, he was getting ready for what the thought was his upcoming honeymoon," Mom answered.

I smiled when it hit me where Mom was going with this. Celia smiled, too. It made total sense.

DC noticed me smiling and said, "I guess I'm the only one who doesn't get it yet."

"He was taking Altonquin," Mom explained, "and if

you ask Googles what the side effects are, you'll find it's something a man would want to do on his honeymoon."

I could hear the sound of eavesdroppers reaching for the cell phones to search out the effects of the medication. Judging by the titters, they'd discovered what side effect the medicine had on Mr. Sanders.

DC gave a slight chuckle and nodded. "But can you prove it, Jo?"

"I bet if you fingerprint the capsules, you'll find most of them have Harold's prints on them and very few will have Celia's."

"And how do you figure that?" DC asked.

"She only gave him medicine when he needed to take it. She didn't need to touch every pill in the bottle, only the pills he would swallow. He knew she'd insist on taking his medicine, but he didn't want the side effects to derail his honeymoon fun. So he poured out most of the medicine to lower his dosage, putting his fingerprints all over those pills. The poor man probably didn't even know he was poisoned. He likely thought he'd taken too little of his medication. So when he first felt the symptoms of his death, he reached for his medicine to take some. That's why the pills were spilled all over the floor."

Celia burst into applause. "That was just like Sherlock Holmes!" she said. At first I was taken aback, but she was so confident with her clapping Wenling joined her and soon the entire restaurant applauded. I glanced over to Jess. Her friends clapped, but she didn't. I looked over to Celia, and she raised her eyebrows and smiled at me. She'd noticed, too.

Mom reached over my lap, took her purse out of the chair next to me, and motioned for him to join our table. DC smiled and sat down. He leaned over to me and said, "Your Mom's an impressive lady."

"I know," I said back.

"It runs in the family," he said and winked. It is a rare man who can pull off a wink without looking cheesy, and DC Cooper was that man. My heart jumped into my throat, but I think I played it cool.

Todd excused himself to write the story, and we all had dinner.

"Ready for dessert?" Mom asked. "Celia's buying ice cream."

"You know what I could go for," DC said. "Another slice of that mango cake. You gave me a slice at the party to take home, and I've been craving it ever since."

"That's a good idea," Celia said, happy to get out of buying us all ice cream, I'm sure.

I hadn't had one slice of mango cake since I'd moved back home. "I'll go get it from the kitchen," I volunteered.

"I'll help," Wenling said.

We both headed for the kitchen to grab plates and cakes. Wenling sent a busboy over to refill the drinks and clear the dinner dishes.

"Such a fun night!" Wenling said to me. "Your mother has a head for mystery."

"It's like a party," I said. Then it struck me that Wenling might know something about the briefcase. "Does Mom suspect there was foul play regarding Aunt Lalaine?"

"She does," Wenling said.

"I thought Aunt Lalaine died in a car accident."

"No accident," Wenling said. "Your Mom thinks it has to do with the family inheritance."

"Grandpa was an artist. We didn't have an inheritance," I said.

Wenling shook her head no. "Your grandmother's family was very rich. She died when your Mom was young. Your mother's aunts cheated her, and your Aunt Lalaine and Mom were suing them. Then just before the case went to trial, which took years, your aunt died. Your mother doesn't think it was a coincidence."

"She never told me," I said.

"You were too young," Wenling said.

"Why didn't Mom pursue it later?" I asked.

"The judge was paid off. Some important documents went missing. Money was too tight for your mother to travel all the way back to The Philippines to solve it. Then, your father got sick. She just couldn't afford to follow up. She says she might do it when her pension checks kick in."

"Or if we make a go of the catering business," I said.

Before Wenling could say anything, Mom came into the kitchen. "What's the holdup? Everyone wants some mango cake! Even the other customers."

"Looks like we might sell out," Wenling said with a smile, as we carried out one cake for our table and handed the waiters slices for the customers.

We all ate, drank, and made merry, now that the murder was solved.

One of the restaurant patrons stopped at the table. She looked familiar, but I didn't know her name. Naturally Mom knew her.

"Jo," she said, "I think I could use your help. I think someone in our office has been leaking information to —"

"That sounds like a matter for the police," DC interrupted. "These ladies are not licensed investigators."

"It's just a hunch. It's too early to get the police involved, but I guess you're right," she said.

Mom looked disappointed, and even though DC was right, I was mad at him for spoiling Mom's fun. The woman nodded and headed for the door, when an idea hit me. I got up from the table and rushed to catch her.

"Excuse me," I said. She stopped. "We might not be licensed investigators, but we are licensed caterers. Perhaps, if you were to throw an office party, it would give Mom and me an excuse to look around, and a way to interview your employees without them knowing. We couldn't guarantee anything, but--"

"That'll work. I'm desperate, and the last company I worked for hired an investigator, and then the investigator sold information. Not to mention what kind of message hiring an investigator would send to our board," she said, shuffling in her purse. "I'll make up an excuse for a party and you two can come in." She pulled her business card out of her purse and handed it to me. "Call me tomorrow, and we'll set it up. Budget isn't an issue. I need to get to the bottom of this."

I returned to the table. DC was giving me the side eye.

"What's up, kid?" Mom asked.

I looked down at the card and said, "Barbara Turing

of Turing Tech is having an office party she needs us to cater."

I avoided eye contact with DC, and Mom smiled. And that's how we got our second case.

Even though DC wasn't too happy with me for getting that catering gig, he still smiled at me before he left. Celia drove her car home to sleep in her own bed for the night, and Wenling had two of the staff stay late to clean up, so she didn't need our help.

Mom packed up the leftovers, and we headed home in the van.

I pulled up to our house, and I realized for the first time in over six years, I felt like I was home. "Great job tonight, Sherlock," I told Mom.

Mom smiled and unlocked the front door. "You're the Sherlock," she said.

We walked into the house, and I tripped over our new cat.

"That cat is out to get me," I said, as Mom crouched down to pet him. I folded my legs and scooted over to the cat. I got two pets in before his ears went back. "What are we going to call him?" I asked.

"Moriarty," Mom said. "Because he's your nemesis."

I laughed. My furry nemesis might be named Moriarty, but deep down I knew Mom was the Sherlock of our crime duo.

I wanted to ask Mom about Aunt Lalaine, but she looked so content petting Moriarty. I vowed to give Barbara a call tomorrow and make sure she ordered a lot of food. Whatever was going on with the suitcase in the closet, more money would help.

"Kid," Mom said, not looking up and continuing to pet the cat. "I know you feel weird about moving back home, but it's true when I tell people you're helping me."

I didn't bother asking Mom how she knew how I'd been feeling. I'd figured it out. Mom knew so much about people because she paid attention. I needed to do that more.

———

MORE MOM AND CHRISTY MYSTERIES!

MOM AND CHRISTY HAVE ANOTHER CASE! ALL they need to do is find out who is selling secrets to Turing Tech's competitor. And being caterers, a party is the perfect cover for snooping (and a legal way to get paid). There's just one problem.

Their prime suspect winds up dead, and their new client, Barbara Turing, is arrested for his murder. Can they prove she's innocent? Find out how they crack the case in Apple Pies and Alibis.

A NOTE FROM THE AUTHOR (AND HER MOM)

M om and I finished running errands, and we popped into Denny's for a quick lunch.

"I'm working on a book about a daughter and her Filipina mom who solve mysteries," I told her. "The mom's named Jo, and the daughter's named, Christy."

Mom laughed. "You should write a book about the manangal. Make it like Stephen King. People like Stephen King."

Mom ordered her eggs and lamented that we hadn't gotten to Denny's before they stopped serving grits. I ordered a burger. The waitress dropped off Mom's coffee, and my diet soda.

Mom told me more about the manangal, a creature from Filipino folklore. He's a pretty scary dude, who doesn't have a body. He's just a floating head with intestines hanging from his head.

"He'll beat you with his intestines," Mom explained. She talked about being on a camping trip and thinking the mosquito net would protect her from the monster, but her friend told her the manangal can go through the net like a ghost. The manangal didn't show that night.

I told her about the mother and daughter in my book. "The mom watches crime shows, and the daughter has a very accurate memory."

"Your memory isn't that good."

"It's fiction like Sherlock Holmes, but there's cake and stuff."

Mom thought about it for a minute and took a sip from her coffee. "So you're Watson, and I'm Sherlock."

"Why can't I be Sherlock?"

"Watson is the one that writes it down."

I laughed. Then my mind flipped back to all the things my mother has figured out over the years–all the little mysteries in life. And then I remembered the big mysteries she solved and wondered how I'd never written about an amateur detective Mom sooner. Every mother is part detective!

MUCH LIKE THE CHARACTER IN MY BOOK, I'VE realized Mom is always right. So, I may have to write a book about the manangal. In the meantime, I'll continue writing about how fictional Mom and I solve mysteries.

FOR THE RECORD, I HAVE AN OLDER SISTER (whose cat Puddin' looks and acts a lot like Moriarty) and a younger brother. Being the middle child, I didn't give them big parts in this first book because I wanted to hog fictional mom's attention.

I HOPE YOU ENJOYED THIS SHORT, INTRODUCTORY mystery. Reviews help other readers decide if they want to buy a book, even short ones. Please review this book if you if can. To find out about upcoming books, get free advanced copies of new cozies, special discounts, fun extras (like cute pics of the cat that inspired Moriarty), and more.

JOIN MOM & CHRISTY'S COZY Mysteries Club

Click or copy and paste this link into your browser:

http://christymurphy.com/club

72677054R00091

Made in the USA
Middletown, DE
07 May 2018